REPTILE HOUSE

WINNER OF THE BOA SHORT FICTION PRIZE

D1051716

WITHDRAWN

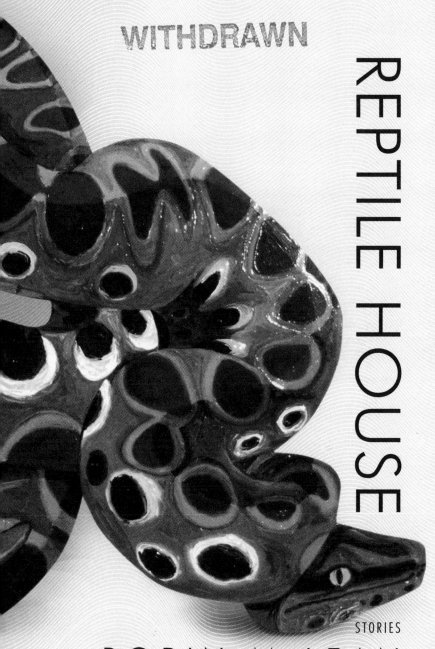

REPTILE HOUSE

STORIES

ROBIN McLEAN

AMERICAN READER SERIES, NO. 24

BOA Editions, Ltd. ❧ Rochester, NY ❧ 2015

Copyright © 2015 by Robin McLean
All rights reserved
Manufactured in the United States of America

First Edition
15 16 17 18   7 6 5 4 3 2 1

For information about permission to reuse any material from this book please
contact The Permissions Company at www.permissionscompany.com or e-mail
permdude@eclipse.net.

Publications by BOA Editions, Ltd.—a not-for-profit
corporation under section 501 (c) (3) of the United States
Internal Revenue Code—are made possible with funds
from a variety of sources, including public funds from the
New York State Council on the Arts, a state agency; the
Literature Program of the National Endowment for the
Arts; the County of Monroe, NY; the Lannan Foundation
for support of the Lannan Translations Selection Series;
the Mary S. Mulligan Charitable Trust; the Rochester Area
Community Foundation; the Arts & Cultural Council
for Greater Rochester; the Steeple-Jack Fund; the Ames-
Amzalak Memorial Trust in memory of Henry Ames,
Semon Amzalak and Dan Amzalak; and contributions from many individuals
nationwide. See Colophon on page 200 for special individual acknowledgments.

ART WORKS.
arts.gov

State of the Arts

NYSCA

Cover Design: Sandy Knight
Interior Design and Composition: Richard Foerster
Manufacturing: Versa Press, Inc.
BOA Logo: Mirko

Library of Congress Cataloging-in-Publication Data

McLean, Robin.
Reptile House / Robin McLean. — First Edition.
    pages cm. — (American Reader Series, No. 24)
ISBN 978-1-938160-65-3 (pbk. : alk. paper) — ISBN 978-1-938160-66-0 (ebook)
I. Title.
PS3613.C5774R47 2015
813'.6—dc23
                                        2014040140

BOA Editions, Ltd.
250 North Goodman Street, Suite 306
Rochester, NY 14607
www.boaeditions.org
A. Poulin, Jr., Founder (1938–1996)

For Mom and Dad

Contents

Cold Snap

In December, the valley cars barely turned over. Batteries died. Blankets were coiled on the sills of frosted windows, tacked over ill-fitting doors. Wood split with a tap of an axe. The ice on the lake was three feet thick, then five, then seven, then the auger froze. When the wind died down, the townsfolk had parties on the lake below the Ledges, the deepest part of the lake, so warmest water, so best fishing. The fish huts all huddled together. The friends built fires in the middle of pallets with brush hauled out in trucks parked behind the huts. The fire was taller than the roofs. It leaned with the wind. They drank hot drinks with gloves, red noses at rims, leaned away from the lick of flame. Their boots shuffled and stamped toes awake; winter's good fun when it's a real winter. They breathed steam around hats and muffs, told jokes across the fire, clapped mitts and laughed hard about the cold snap.

Lilibeth could see all from the boat launch. The party was a mile away from the windshield. She chewed chicken salad from the deli counter. She bobbed her head to the oldies station the next valley over, which cut out while her head bobbed on. This chicken was good. Its plastic bin balanced on the steering wheel so her gloves were free. She'd gotten the binoculars in the divorce. She chewed and watched the huddle move around the flame melting a crater in the ice: no danger in this cold, but what did the fish think? The light, the shapes. Some coming disaster. The lake aboil. The crater would freeze smooth, always did, with charred sticks, broken glass, and bark swimming in it. She'd lost the fish hut in the divorce, but the gambrel roofline was distinctive. She squinted for it in the lenses, but fish huts all look the same at twilight.

Last winter had been warm, so they weren't expecting it. The mercury dropped every day. In town, at the school and meeting places, they talked ozone holes and natural cycles and getting suckered by headlines. They wore wool socks. They ordered extra blankets from catalogues.

It got colder still. The furnace ran 24/7 at the Food Boy, the only store in the valley with a deli and pharmacy section. The snow machiners bought no gas. The station owners groused. The men stayed in and finally painted the babies' rooms and fixed the drips in basements. Easter Creek froze, the ice dammed up, then the creek burst and overflowed the dam, until the dam broke loose and took Smitty's Bridge out.

"That bridge was too low anyway," people said, taking pictures. "That bridge had it coming."

The Town Council voted on the bridge. The road crew erected a fence and sign as directed, then the wind came up and flung the fence in the creek and the sign high up in a downstream tree, *Road Closed! Go Back!* which they thought was funny and took more pictures. They voted again, a second resolution, calling for a less casual effort, for concrete blocks, no dirt work was possible, secured with reliable knots to reliable trees. The Town Clerk should have arranged the work, but broke his leg the next morning. Lilibeth found him sprawled on black ice, called the ambulance, yelled "Hello!" and waved them into Elm Street. She'd been walking her dogs. Further resolutions were tabled when the pipes froze in Town Hall.

Lilibeth had once known all the resolutions. She used to take minutes, a public service, given her handwriting. But since the divorce she'd been lying low. She lived with the dogs in a house on the hump of the hill in the middle of Elm Street. The chickens lived in the shed. The house fit her budget and was tucked in the pines, which leaned so far the house was nearly invisible. Electric wires dropped down to the roof through branches and needles. The pines hardly swayed in greatest gusts. Her new address was not yet added to the Newsletter list, so she was not up on things.

The valley got colder. The pipes froze downtown in the houses and shops on Main Street. The houses up on the hills and slopes lasted longer due to thermal inversions. On the lake, the drifts climbed the fish huts, ramped up the walls until the kids off school could scramble to the roofs then slide back down again and again, their mothers watching from idling cars, calling out "enough!" when they thought about frostbite. At night, the drifts wrapped around the sides until only the doors that opened inward opened at all. One kid stayed overnight on a dare. They tried to cut him out in the morning. The mother was frantic. The oil plugged the chainsaws. The handsaws' blades snapped in two. The heads of mauls dropped off their handles. Such was the freezing differential between ash wood and steel.

"It's too cold to keep trying," the police chief said since it was too late anyway. "You people go home." They all did but the mother.

Many went to the fire hall. They huddled around the radio. The broadcast died during the lead-in: post office frozen three towns north.

"POs should be immune," they agreed at an emergency meeting. "Given federal regulations on pipe depth."

"The plumbers must be making a mint," they said as backup generators hummed.

The price of stove wood went sky high. Families played board games together for the first time in years.

When the broadcast died, Lilibeth was listening in a bathtub not deep or fancy, but hot and reliable. Her dad had bought the radio in Hong Kong in the service. It was top of the line in its time. She'd got it in probate. She got out of the tub to shake it. She dripped on the floor, which was cold on her feet.

She'd gotten the house cheap, a foreclosure, as-is. It needed paint. The porch sagged, with mice in the crawlspace, but the furnace was good as were the roof and well. She jiggled the toilet handle, which was running nonstop again. The plumber had not called back yet. She brought the phone to the edge of the tub and got back in. She'd given Norm her number weeks ago, a fireman. It was his idea despite his wife's death last year. Norm was a shy one. He had only one friend outside the crew, an old miner.

Lilibeth splashed.

She'd met the old miner once on Norm's doorstep. They'd popped by Norm's at the same time. Lilibeth rang the bell. The old miner carried a tray with a turkey.

"I need the oven," the old miner had said when Norm appeared.

The turkey was pink, freshly plucked, and pimpled. The old miner stepped in past Lilibeth, searched for salt and pepper, took a shower. He slept on a rug by the wood stove as the turkey roasted.

Turkey scent filled Norm's house just as Lilibeth was leaving.

"That old boy will be the last man standing," Norm had said.

The miner's face glowed in the firelight. He was very thin, but used no blanket.

"I don't know about that," Lilibeth had said.

In the bath, she watched the phone when not watching her knees, which were islands washed in the tropical sea with hot foamy bubbles. The washcloth was a baby eel, which dove around coral reefs, her calves, ankles, and thighs. She dried her hands and pressed a few digits of Norm's number. She did not understand. She set the phone down. She'd turned up the thermostat in the hallway and the furnace rumbled. "Let the man come to you," the book said. "Never push a man or he'll head for the hills. A man likes to feel in charge."

The pines tapped the roof gently as the wind whipped and arched over Elm Street and everywhere.

"We've never seen such a cold snap," they said when Fish and Game closed. "Till the road gets better," the Game Warden said. Some went to Florida. Roads drifted in over notches and passes. Some wells had hand pumps and people pumped into buckets until their eyelashes stuck together. The ice on the lake was twenty feet deep according to the high school science club, which met anyway.

Tree limbs snapped power lines, candles burned low, and oil tanks emptied. Animals made dens. Emergency meetings served hot chocolate and sweet rolls. Birds tucked away somewhere. School closed for another week. Story time moved to the fire hall for the littlest kids. The engine bays had never been fuller. The kids loved the ladders and pole from the bunk room and the first-aid kit was near at hand. The firemen peed down by the creek where the bridge had been, jogged down through trees in full gear and masks.

"Someone will forget and drive right off that," one said. His beard was ice.

"Even lawyers need to eat," another said. They zipped up quick and jogged back through trees again. Masks fogged then cleared, fogged then cleared.

Town Council resolved to call the tank farm two valleys over for additional oil trucks. They were told to call the Capitol and left messages. The fire hall was busy. They ate on paper plates around the blower. The dogs chased the cups that cart-wheeled away.

"This is fun!" the kids said.

"The capital N in Nature," the librarian said.

The leach fields and septic tanks were soon rock solid, then septic lines. Old outhouses were cleared of shrubs grown in. Others rolled trashcans to the edge of decks with curtains around them. Holes were cut in the seats of wicker chairs and buckets placed under. This was hardest on the sick, elderly, and shy. City fathers looked the other way. They'd decide on the collection and disposal at next Town Meeting.

Lilibeth read like a scholar. The books on self-improvement were stacked by her bed. Her TV had been broken since her last boyfriend. It sat on the porch as if looking for the street. He'd kicked the screen in, a sheriff's deputy-in-training. Maybe Norm felt a conflict of interest that she'd dated a fellow man in uniform. She did not understand. Until the radio died, she'd not missed the TV.

She took baths while reading. She took baths and filled out job applications. Norm's wife was the most likely reason. "He needs time before his next commitment," the book on grief said. "Don't be overeager during the healing phase," another said, "Soul-mating takes time." He'd suggested she trim back the pines, a fire hazard. "I like the closed-in feeling," she'd told him. He had not offered his chainsaw though he was certified. It had been their one night together.

Things could always be better. The warning light in her car was a little golden engine. The guy from the shop had not called back. She tried to remember if she owed him money. The trees around her house seemed bigger and thicker in this cold, to lean down like a tent. She'd missed her period, and though the test was negative, her message no doubt had upset Norm. When she ventured out with job applications, his car was at the fire hall, not his normal shift. The parking lot was full, some party, the faces and heads behind the frost of the roll-up glass of engine bays. She pulled in and watched. Some people waved at her. Even her ex-truck was parked there, the one with the hitch to pull the fish hut. She must have forgotten some holiday because all the shops were closed on Main Street. She'd knocked on the glass, "Hello! Hello!" She left the applications in doorways, under flowerpots and stabbed by the edges of shovels. The flag at the cannon in the square had been ripped by the wind. The cars were drifted-in. The meters were red, all out of time, not a single ticket.

She saw a group, a family, and called, "Hello!" The family was so bundled, she could not be sure if they were male or female. A bundled baby swung from a parent's hip, its small face crushed to the larger shoulder, perhaps crying over a frostbitten nose or ice-cold feet or numbed earlobes. She squatted to study their stampede of tracks. They turned down an alley. They never turned. She nearly felt their heat under an awning, almost sniffed their smell around a corner. She followed for a while, then she looped back to the square past the antique shop and hardware store.

It felt colder in town than at her house. She stamped her boots and hugged her arms. It felt much colder. She marveled at this impression. How real it seemed, how actual, factual, reliable, true. How apparently based on sensory perception, the nerves in the face, for example, the capillaries of the ears when the hat flew off and tumbled away. The pain in the lungs, deep breaths required for catching the hat, for leaping a drift.

She stood at the flag by the cannon. She folded the last application and stuffed it in her pocket. She would have to rewrite it. The chase had rumpled it terribly. Her car rumbled and puffed all alone by the library, and she marveled at the power of the mind, since she knew from her readings that such impressions of doom were purely psychological: mere exaggerations of the current conditions caused by the scar tissues of grief—swollen up layers of disappointment, sadness and anger, the book said, which ganged up to distort perception, to disable the afflicted. Don't believe this empty town. This coldest cold. This Death of the World.

She wrote her real problems on paper. They hung on the fridge behind a magnet. She studied the list while eating soup from a can at the oven door, open to 350°:

> Mice in crawlspace.
> Percolator plug / missing / lost.
> Woodpile low / get wood
> Dogs tracking bark into house
> Dogs chewing braided rug
> Engine light / engine light
> Chicken feed
> Find job / anything
> Toaster adjustment

When the bath started acting up, she added it below: Bath / coughing / investigate.

There were other issues: In the morning, she found the chickens huddled together under the light bulb. They were not happy. They pecked each other out of boredom and stress, the chicken book said. She dabbed cream between feathers on the scabby parts. She told them to simmer down, look on the sunny side. Things are always worse for someone else. Her snow pants pockets needed patching, for example. Quarters fell out and anything smaller. Her phone card minutes ran to zero. She lost the charger for her phone, so how could the shops call for an interview? She drove down Main to add notes about the charger. Her applications still flapped in the doorways. The extended new holiday apparently continued. She would buy a calendar after her first paycheck.

The plumber's office door was open. She left a note on the desk chair about the tub. "I can't live without it."

When the hand pumps froze, people filled their jugs at the Easter Hill Spring, an old pipe in the slope that poured out constantly. The plows cleared the pullout to it. The pipe was the width of a thumb. It filled a cistern built by a Water Committee decades back. A historical plaque said some old miner dug the spring out for his mules.

"It's artesian," some Committee members had argued.

"Geothermal," said the ones who'd been to college.

"It's God either way," said the religious faction. "The Flock will not go thirsty."

During the cold snap, they kept a fire burning by the spring. Each family backed in with empty jugs and a stick of wood they threw on the fire. Kids tapped the fire's edges with their boots. As the cold pressed in, the pipe lengthened and thickened with days and weeks, until the ice on the pipe was an elephant's trunk with a smirky tip where wind had shaped it and the water dripped out. Some women wouldn't look at it. Men and boys made jokes. Exhaust from the tailpipes sank and swirled, and people coughed. They filled buckets and tubs and screw-top jars. They dragged the heaviest through snow to tailgates. Birds landed on the cistern and were shooed away. Town dogs licked the runoff.

Once, Lilibeth pulled in at the pullout to see about the hubbub: cars abandoned, jumper cables hanging out, water jugs half-buried. She waved at friends she'd not seen for ages. She shook her head and mouthed her question. "No water?" her lips said. "I've got water at my house!" Her eyes and teeth were big and her mittens excited as they pointed toward Elm Street. The friends tapped on windows too iced up to roll down and pointed at their phones. "On the line to the Capitol," their lips said, and Lilibeth nodded as if she understood they were requesting reinforcements, water trucks and propane rations, a generator at school so the kids did not fall behind.

Sometimes she'd have liked to hurl a rock: to coil the arm, to let fly at glass, but it was hard to justify such an idea.

The old friends waved goodbye. They gave thumbs up with empty milk jugs. A show of support, she thought later, for finally getting up and running, surviving her troubles, like writing GO TEAM GO! on the glass.

The plumber didn't show. Norm didn't call. The little golden engine on the car's console was now a constant. The town's sudden holiday must have been extended. Days dropped away and away. The sink and toilet were fine, but now the tub was failing. It sputtered a tepid twisting trickle. It groaned as if giving in. Water boiled in pots to supplement, in the kitchen, on the wood stove. She dumped hot over the cold sheen of bubble bath. She stirred the mixture and got in with a book about self-employment, but who could dream with all this worry? In the morning, she drove to the plumber's house. The door was open, "Hello!" The fire hall lot was empty, the weeks-long party was over. All engines gone. The school was dark. The library drop box was frozen shut. She kept the books.

Capitol Radio reported frost to twenty-two feet. All Governor's staff was in the emergency bunker, well-stocked, but the pantry bunker froze. The canned goods were crushed, oozed when heated. The staff cooks asked to bring their children down, but with so little space no one else was permitted. Rivers froze to the bottom. Dams iced in. Rail lines snapped at critical junctions. Coal cars stood in the western fields. Southern news crews showed footage of icicles, people chipping, sucking, so thirsty, so thirsty.

When she found the hardware store ajar, she borrowed a crowbar and a bag of mousetraps. She pried the back library door. She easily found the plumbing book section.

First step, the book said, was locate the blockage. The crawlspace was low and dirty with mouse droppings. She crouched at the door. She crawled lower as the ground sloped up. She baited the mousetraps with peanut butter.

Mapping the kitchen sink was easy with the pencil. She crawled along the copper to the first major junction and marked it. The flashlight shone up on the belly of the house where the junction split. She followed the split to the bathroom sink, to the toilet, to the place where the tub sagged down like a cave explorer. She lay crushed under floor joists, barely room to pull a mitten off, to feel for the frozen place.

She crawled out and boiled water. She crawled back under with a paintbrush. There was no room for pouring. She painted the pipe with scalding water in the beam of the flashlight. The blockage was enormous, a foot across at least of frosty copper, and the brushed-on water was no match for it. She went to bed dry and cold.

Days and nights came and went. She climbed on her car roof to the broken window at Food Boy for peanut butter and dog food, which she also fed the chickens. She left IOUs signed and dated. The aisles were flooded and frozen. She screwed screws down through her boots for extra traction. Her car roof got scratched. She picked any shopping cart she wanted. Back home she lit candles under the blockage and steamy bowls of water. If only she'd tried this hard with marriage, employed creativity. When candles and bowls failed, she lit twigs in the frying pan and slid it under. She added paper slowly, but the flames licked the joists and she doused the pan. "Think with logic for once!" she wrote in her journal and thought how if she froze, her ex would come to identify the body. Who else would do it? He'd flip through this journal on the kitchen table. He'd see how much she had learned, how substantial she'd become from new experience, how far she'd advanced as a human being. After the fire, the tub coughed rusty drops that she tried to analyze.

She tried innovations. She bent a hanger straight and shoved it in. She banged the faucet with a hammer, but chipped the tile. She tried the hammer in the crawlspace too, but made no headway without any backswing. She set the mice on the woodpile for the birds. She washed her hair in the kitchen sink with a mug poured over her neck. Soapy water ran down her forehead to sink to drain through pipes to tank to leach field, then down, down through pebbles and rocks in layers, between faults toward magma, only to steam up again, spit out someday, maybe some geyser, some national park with buffalo romping and children. Anyway, her hair was clean. She reread an old paper by the wood stove while drying the hair, then burned the paper to prevent rereading.

Some days she crawled under the house and sat with the pipe and the mice. She wished for a weasel, which she understood ate ten mice per day. Sometimes the dogs sat with her. Sometimes the chickens came to be chased by the dogs.

Outside, she stretched. She reset her scarf over her nose. The sky was patches through branches and needles. Not a puff of wind. Birds pecking frozen seeds.

She drove to the lake with the little gold engine beaming. She parked at the boat launch. She walked across the ice over ten-foot drifts and slid down the back sides, then bare patches, on and on. The ice groaned sometimes, made lines and cracks in spider webbing. Pine branches had blown and impaled themselves upright in drifts, such tender new forests, so sudden and stupid.

She walked to the fish huts. She circled the fire crater. She peered in windows. When she found her old fish hut, the door opened to the armchair. Fishhooks stabbed up the armrests. A fish was penciled on the wall—Bass, 8 lbs, the date under it—and a picture of the ex with a girl and a girl with a fish hooked from gills and thumb. A jigsaw puzzle glued together. She tugged the handle of the door in the floor. The skin of ice was thin. She bashed it in with the pick leaning on the cooler.

"Hello!" she called down.

She tied a hook to a line. She tied the sinker. She sat in the armchair. The beer in the cooler had exploded into aluminum ribbons. She dropped the hook down into deepest waters where it floated in the warm current with the fishes.

As the glaciers moved south toward the Capitol, some high points and valleys were spared. Ice slipped around them, while the rising sea pressed the coastlines. Planes dropped from the sky, no one knew why. Engineers volunteered from the private sector. They repaired and upgraded. They drilled for heat in the earth, hot water or steam, to turn the turbines. It was proven science, but the crews were stressed and components untested. Reactor waters were ice rinks boiling in the middles when the sea crawled up over boardwalks and streets, consuming bike paths and smashing hot-dog stands against shopping districts and schools.

Lilibeth studied copper and drew maps.

Once, she drove to the spring looking for the old miner. She'd seen him there sometimes removing tires from abandoned cars. She honked when she saw him. He wore a leather cap tied under his chin. He dragged a sack through the parking area. He dropped the sack, darted off in the wrong direction, up the hill, his canteen swinging. She ran after him for a while up through the trees, but this slope was difficult. How did the old man do it? On the steepest pitches she clawed on hands and knees, but this old miner was very fast. Sometimes she stopped to spit, to call toward the ridge top, "Wait for me!"

The sack contained a half-skinned opossum, a snare and fishhooks. She studied how he'd done the skinning. She kicked the snow for his knife. She took the sack.

She called the plumber again, then Norm once more, then threw the phone in a dumpster behind Fish and Game.

Back home, she walked the TV to the curb. Her neighbors' trash was no better than hers, a sanitation strike she guessed. She'd so lost track of current events. She blew on her gloves. The dogs ran around while she wandered the trash. She dragged a couch down Elm Street. On the corner she found a three-bladed fan on a pedestal base with an oscillating cage. She walked it home and ate dinner with the fan across the table.

She found an extension cord in the hardware store. She plugged the cord in on the porch and dragged it all around to the crawlspace. It was almost night time when she tried it. The flashlight wagged. The mice scattered.

The fan wedged between the ground and joists, as close as could be to the blockage. She dialed the oscillation off to focus all energy and clicked the fan on. The three blades hummed like moths on the window. She took a nap.

She took chicken from the freezer to celebrate. She boiled rice in a pot and shared it with the dogs like a party. The fan purred below. She filled the tub, hot and fast, peeled off everything, and sank into a miracle; the tangible principles of airflow science she'd never learned in school, the kinetics of wind, surely, derivative of planetary motion, most likely, solar storms flared millions of miles arriving at the earth eight minutes later, parting like water around a stone in a creek, excited atoms in thinnest atmosphere bumping and shoving the next bunch down, again and again. Atoms prevail! Comprehension so overrated! The healing phase very truly takes time. Don't push Lilibeth or she'll head for the hills! Lilibeth likes to feel she's in charge!

She soaked until the book was soaked when she woke, her bottom teeth under. She spit out and toweled off.

The next day she walked the thermometer to the curb, stuck at minus 75 for weeks, more proof of cheap modern manufacturing. She stitched her snowpants. She walked the fan to the car and turned the ignition. She aimed the blades through the steering wheel at the little golden engine. She cracked a window and napped. When she woke the car started right up. She drove to town. The fan sat in the passenger seat.

At the library, she borrowed volcano stories and Spanish grammar in case she and Norm ever got to Mexico. A sign at the gas station said, "Take What You Need," so she filled the tank.

In the square, sandbags lay scattered where they had fallen off some speeding vehicle. A truck was turned over against the cannon. The sandbags looked like kids at naptime under small brown blankets. She carried several to her trunk for traction.

"Hello!" she called.

The rope of the flag clanged the pole. Keep trying. Keep trying. She drove to the dumpster behind Fish and Game and climbed in. Her phone was right on top.

"Hello!" she called from atop the dumpster. "Hello! Hello! Hello!"

The waves of her sound rolled down the lake. The words bounced to shore and up the slopes and ricocheted off a glacier dammed in the next valley over. When her voice hit the ice, it bounced back down: "Hello! Hello! Hello!" it said. Though the words were smaller, they were distinct and friendly. This new blue wall made the ridges look silly.

Her neck ached from gazing. She memorized the new skyline.

She drove by Norm's house one last time. His car was parked at the curb and a deputy's cruiser was parked in the driveway. Both drivers' doors were wide open. All Norm's tires were missing and the cruiser's were flat. She walked the perimeter of the cruiser with the fan. If the tires inflated, it was very slowly.

The smell of wood smoke was unmistakable.

"Hello!" she called at the door. "This is your last chance!"

She used a rock to break the window. The wood stove stood in the middle of the living room. She circled it. The fire was low with bark and papers. The old miner from the spring lay bundled on the hearth, filthy and ripe, she could smell him from the doorway. She knelt and approached him on hands and knees. When she sniffed him, his eyes opened on her. His tongue circled like a slug along his lips, cracked but still plump and trying to speak. She'd have liked a few questions answered: why'd you run from me, for example. Why did you run? But his lips were down-turned and dismal, prone, it seemed, to gloom and disappointment, though gloom was understandable. Perhaps the spring froze up finally. Perhaps he'd lost his dog. Perhaps Norm had ordered him out of the house. Perhaps he'd quit looking for his dog and family, but how can things improve if you stop the search?

She didn't ask. She wasn't in the mood for gloom. Silence was better.

When his mitten lifted, it pointed for the canteen, and she backed away. His lips sucked. His tongue licked, so thirsty. His canteen lay on the braided rug, the very rug she once told Norm was like her rug at her house, what a pleasing design, what a funny coincidence.

The canteen was a good one, Army surplus. She reeled it in by its cord. She unscrewed the cap.

His mouth spoke in a frozen language. She shushed him with her finger to his lips. She squatted by him like an island, explored the face with her hands, the neck, the shoulders. She found the knife on his belt. The blade was sharp, well cared for. The knife cut with urgency, now telling him: Be quiet, Don't speak, spoke in slicing motions across his neck, not silent, but speechless until his frown was gone. His eyes were wide and she dropped the knife into her bag. She would clean the blade later with snow, between thumb and palm, snap it shut.

She hung the canteen over her shoulder. It sloshed half-full and swung like a toy. Before she left she searched down the cellar steps for supplies. The rooms were smaller than she remembered. Her head seemed to scrape the ceilings, to stoop low under lintels. She'd grown so big and strong. She could have snapped a chair over her knee.

At home, she set the fan to oscillate in every room. She fanned the chickens one by one. They looked like dogs on a ride, so happy and free. She guessed the radio station was Cairo, still garbled weeks after installing the antennae from her neighbor's roof. She had cut down a sapling for better reception.

The chickens would be kinder to each other if spring came, with great bundles of buds to break all records, a bumper crop in the sudden heat and gush of creeks. The leaves would burst open. The turkeys would hatch. "*La piñata fiesta*," she'd pronounce on the porch to pine trunks and to acorns forming tiny, nearly-nothings on stems, in the swirl of the great unfolding green. She sat on the roof with binoculars scanning in all directions. She did not mind waiting.

Take the Car Take the Girl

William had called at five for a table for four at six. He got the best table in the house as usual: the round and white by the bay window, a little apart from the others, facing the street behind the glass and the cars parked at the line of meters. The streetlights had not come on yet. The tablecloth fell off sharp and cast a blue edge on the blond wood floor. As the sun went down, the edge got wider and bluer, and would swallow the restaurant to the back wall.

Tweedy sipped opposite her husband, William, and William talked to Michael on his right, a new man from the Club. Tweedy's hiccups were at eighteen-second intervals. The doctor had given her pills. She needed a refill. Her blouse was pinned at the neck with a sterling bee. Her hiccups were, for the most part, quiet and unoffending. The waiter refilled the wine with a twist of his wrist. He wore black and white and circled like a planet, pouring. He almost bowed in his duties but did not bow, while Tweedy's busboy did seem to bow to the table as he delivered a new shaker of salt. His black pants were so big on his slender frame that the belt cinched tight was required. His white shirt billowed out over the belt. His father's clothes, she thought, or stepfather's. "Can I help you?" she wanted to say, poor thing. This boy needed some petting, anyone could see that. The waiter circled and poured. Her busboy was a beautiful boy, pink and blue in the face, with a basket of bread. At the other tables, he bowed and scraped crumbs into his hand.

Tweedy hiccuped. The waiter said, "More water?" and Tweedy said, "I have some, thank you," but he filled her glass anyway and she hiccuped again.

"Poor dear," said William, glancing at Tweedy. He leaned back toward Michael who was taller than William, thirty pounds lighter, still with a sense of future about him. William grasped at the air when he spoke. He reached at territory across the tablecloth. Michael's hands chopped back. They talked the news of the week: the new trash contract Uptown, the judge off to jail, the council meeting gone so very amiss, bosses gumming the works, and how. The new blueprints of the footprint of the central headquarters were planned by the river with a fountain in the atrium, glass and more glass, a high-rent view. Tweedy hiccuped and sipped. "Poor dear."

"We are awaiting our fourth," William said to the waiter. He nodded at the empty seat at his left. Helene was always late.

"Have you tried holding your breath?" said Michael to Tweedy.

"She tried it in the car," William told him. "Holding her breath hardly ever works for Tweedy."

When Tweedy was a girl she had wanted things like tea parties and lemon cake. Michael straightened his tie. Tweedy dabbed her lips with the cloth napkin, a little smudge, what a shame. She had wanted clean white napkins and a husband with a crown on his head, crystal doorknobs to the powder rooms. Her busboy delivered napkins folded like tents to a table in the back. He was a lovely boy, that busboy.

"The election will be tight, I've heard that said," said Michael to William and they got going about it. The side of Michael's hand chopped the table. His hair was dyed black but his eyebrows were graying.

"I disagree completely," said William. "Murdock will run away with it, I disagree."

"I've heard it from several good sources at the Club," said Michael.

"Well, you are so naive," said William with a smile. "So young still."

"No really! Just think of this, stop and think of this," said Michael.

"Truly, you surprise me," said William.

William went to the men's room. Tweedy asked Michael after his family, what schools, what church, what street? William came back and looked at the door. Tweedy hiccuped after seventeen seconds. William looked at his watch.

"I'm sure she will be here soon," said Tweedy. The men went on and Tweedy counted to fifteen seconds, a downward trend worth tending to. She excused herself to the powder room with a glass of water and her turquoise leather handbag. In a stall she bent over and drank all the water down, her head between her knees, her lips sucking on the far side of the glass. She looked in the mirror, her face, the bee at her neck. Someone else entered, a lady in pink, and they stood side by side in the mirror. Tweedy counted: twenty-four seconds this time.

"I know how to help you," the pink lady said, "Honey and lemon will do the trick every time."

"I'll try it," Tweedy said. Tweedy had tried honey and lemon a week ago, ten years ago, she would try again tomorrow.

The pink lady left.

Tweedy refilled her glass at the faucet. She drank between her legs and coughed. She returned to the table where the men were leaning together like old friends again, or better. It was true love over some debacle in Eureka last Sunday, the crash on some corner, the layoffs, the layout, the lineup of the new team, oh the taxi driver, yes, you should have seen this driver, the colonoscopy, the polyp presumed benign, the re-paving of Main. Their heads were so close, perhaps Michael and William would nuzzle. William would run his hand through Michael's stiff hair. Tweedy hoped so. That would be something worth seeing.

They did not nuzzle. The men sat back. They talked of the new steam room at the Club, all cedar with volcanic rocks from Hawaii, and about Art Beeker who died of an aneurysm. They were just talking to Art Beeker in the steam room last week. William and Michael both snapped their fingers to signify Art gone. No one could cure Art's condition. No one knew. Tweedy dabbed her lips and looked for her busboy. He was bent over at a lady's high-heeled shoe, patent leather and black. He knelt like praying to the shoe while saying something to the lady. He dabbed it with a tenderness she had not seen in years. A miracle. She might have married this skinny busboy.

Helene arrived. Helene was big and blonde, a Viking queen. Once Helene had had a small forest of hair on the right side of her chin. The small forest had suited her. Tweedy thought the spirit of the forest was still with Helene entirely. Men flared their nostrils when they looked at Helene.

"Helene, you look wonderful," said William. He stood and they pecked lips. "How the hell is Jack?" he said. "Too bad he couldn't come." William held her waist just longer than necessary and made introductions to Michael, who flared and blinked Helene up and down.

"So sorry I'm late," said Helene wearing red, a good color for her.

"But now we have you," said William. "That's all we want."

"I could eat a horse," said Helene and sat. "Where ever did you get it?" Helene asked pointing at Tweedy's bee. Tweedy said, "Mother," but that was not true at all. She did not remember where she got her bee. It appeared in her jewelry box one day, exactly how all things come.

"I saw your new car," Helene said.

"Did you?" said William, with a twinkle.

"Very handsome," said Michael.

"Very, very handsome," Tweedy said. "William loves his car."

The candles glowed on the tables across the room. Her busboy skated over the blond wood floor, between the tables in the hum of conversation. His sleeves were rolled up and made all the difference in the world. Then her busboy tripped on the mat near the double doors to the kitchen. The water in his pitcher sloshed up, a tidal wave in his pitcher, but did not spill, not a single drop.

Tweedy hiccuped and Helene said, "Has anyone tried pounding your back yet, dear?"

"That's for coughing," said Tweedy.

"Might not hurt to try," said William.

"Or *BOO!* from behind the door? Have you tried that yet?" asked Helene.

"Not yet," said Tweedy. "I don't mind. And I don't like a startle."

"I've heard vinegar works for hiccups," said Michael.

"Don't be silly," William said. "The doctor gave her some pills for it. She needs a refill."

The others ordered meat and Tweedy ordered salad. She didn't care for food anymore. Her head and arms and lungs were made of food and water. Why feed them? The waiter poured from a new bottle of wine that had a picture on the label of people bending and reaching through vines and leaves. The grapes were tiny circles, the faces were tiny circles. The faces looked as happy as the grapes. Tweedy knew not a single one of the tiny faces in the picture. The bottle seemed black until the flame on the table turned it green. Tweedy unbuttoned and buttoned her cuffs. She stretched her arms out to see if the wrists were even. Irritation of the eardrum can cause the hiccups, her doctor had told her. Carbonation. Standing up too fast, crying too loudly. She rubbed her ear. The river was rising. She checked her turquoise handbag. The bottle was still empty.

She stood with the handbag and went back to the powder room for another try at upside-down. Her busboy was lifting dishes from a vacated table to his tray. The tray was wide and heavy, too heavy, how could he? She passed him at the powder room door. He staggered, poor thing, and she did not help him with his dishes since helping a busboy with his dishes would not look right. He disappeared through the swinging doors to the kitchen. He should have a name. Someone in the kitchen might feed him. Someone should.

The doctor had said this: lack of water, too much water, eating too fast, laughing too hard, coughing too much, talking too much, burping, crying too loud. In the powder room she had forgotten the glass of water so she drank with her nose in the sink.

"It's just math," William was saying to Michael when she returned. "Simple math."

"But the broader considerations!" Michael said. "Just think!"

"No reason to fuss so," Helene said to William in a voice that petted his hot red neck.

"Hogwash," said William.

"But you miss my point entirely! Miss my point," Michael said. "Don't you see?"

"I am not missing your point in the least," said William.

Helene pressed William's arm. "Come now."

The doctor had said this too: lack of oxygen, lack of vitamins, clearing one's throat, overstretching one's neck, spicy food.

Tweedy cleared her throat. "I hope it's not spicy."

"Hogwash," said William and pulled his arm from Helene.

Michael moved the salt and pepper around and around each other.

"Is this about the car?" Tweedy said. "William's beautiful car?

"Of course not," said William.

"It's about math," said Michael.

They all laughed about it.

Dinner came, they ate dinner. Tweedy ate her salad like a rabbit. Michael held his knife in the right and his fork in the left. "I picked this up in Europe," he said, showing his teeth. He bit at the fork and not the meat at all. William's fork stood vertical while he chewed. His knife stayed in his hand. He spoke to Helene when he was done chewing. The street was dark outside the window. The streetlights had come on. People passing made dull shapes behind the glass. The food was stiff and bland. At the head of a nearby table, a man with a roasted chicken spilled wine on a lady's lap and the others at the table all groaned, "Oh dear," "What a shame," and handed napkins over. They gripped their glasses tighter and she blotted the split, the dip between her legs, and the busboy blushed when he took the napkins from the lady's lap. He took the glass and the bundle away. Her busboy's name might be Lawrence or Edgar or Geoffrey, tall and slender. The man with the roasted chicken told a story: there was man with no car who hitched rides by waving a gas can at oncoming cars.

"Gas Can Eddie," said the man with the chicken. "This red can. I picked him up myself, no kidding."

Everyone at the table laughed. "Think of a life like that," someone said.

"A life like that," Tweedy said. "A good life too." She might have married that man with the roasted chicken. She might walk over and sit on his knee. It would take ten seconds.

"No kidding," said a man. "Absolutely no kidding here."

Helene told Tweedy of a girl on the news who had hiccups for five weeks straight. "They did shock therapy to stop it."

The busboy brought more bread. The waiter poured. Michael asked William about the mayor's right-hand man, a gesture of peace, and about paving the car park at the Club, which had been William's pride and joy along with the backstabbing contractors, backscratching in back rooms, snake-in-the-grass amendments and substitutions, amen for asphalt. They chewed and chewed. William offered Helene a roll. Helene bit the roll tenderly at him and crumbs fell. Tweedy set her fork down. Her busboy came with his bronze wand. Once at a fondue dinner for eight, Helene had dropped a thick crust of bread from her fork into the bubbling cheese. With William on her right, they, according to the rules, had kissed. It was a good kiss and everyone watched it. Tweedy would give William to Helene if she could think of a graceful way to do it.

"You cannot imagine how smooth it drives," William said leaning toward Helene.

"I've always dreamed of a spin in one," Helene said. She leaned back toward William.

"It's an excellent car, I admit," Michael said to Helene. "An outstanding car."

"An astonishing car," Tweedy said.

"Tonight," William said to Helene. "We'll take you in the car." He dropped the car keys by her plate. "We'll take a spin. Take you home."

"Can I drive it?" said Helene.

"Of course," said William.

"Three's a crowd," said Tweedy. "Perhaps Michael will take me home."

"Shifting's a breeze with this transmission," Michael said to Helene.

"This transmission's new from previous models," said William to Michael.

"Of course," said Michael.

"The absolute most recent transmission," Tweedy said. "Who wouldn't love it?"

"Oh, I don't know," said Helene, as if driving this car was simply not possible. A dream that simply could not come true.

Tweedy picked up the keys. She set the keys in Helene's lap.

"But it is possible," Tweedy said. "Every dream can come true. As they told us as children."

Tweedy had once tried it with another man. They had walked between the trees in the park, he read her poetry with his eyes welling as if the rhymes made sense to him: a Springer Spaniel of a man, that park, those trees, how silly. Once the man left his shirt at the house. Tweedy washed and ironed it, then hung the shirt in William's closet by mistake. She found the shirt sprawled on the bed soon after with a note pinned, "Dear, this is not my size in the arms. Thanks, W."

"So delicious, all of it," said Tweedy. "Not spicy at all."

William waved to the waiter, "I think we're done here."

But what had the Spaniel worn home? It had been fall and windy, too cold without a shirt. She had never thought of it. The busboy came with Tweedy's turquoise handbag. He set it on the tablecloth. "It was found in the powder room," he said, and Tweedy set the handbag in her lap and said, "Oh my goodness, thank you."

"Oh dear," said Helene.

"It must have happened a thousand times," said William to the busboy.

Everyone smiled. "What a darling," said Tweedy and snapped the turquoise mouth open and shut. Took a tissue.

Her busboy went away.

"What's that busboy doing in the powder room anyway?" Michael said. He glared at the busboy's slender back.

"Part of his duties, no doubt," said Helene. "Some check-list or other."

"Nothing sinister," William said.

"Better check you haven't been robbed," Michael said to Tweedy. "Youths these days will do anything."

"That boy?" Tweedy said and opened the bag again. "What could he want from me?" She rummaged through the handbag without looking. "That boy doesn't even have a name."

William snapped at the waiter, "Yes, we are done here, sir." William pointed at the cluttered table and the waiter snapped at the busboy who was drinking water in the back of the restaurant by the kitchen doors. The busboy set the glass on an empty tray. Tweedy watched him weave through: Milton was a good name for the boy, a possibility. Or Pieter Van Something or Martin O'Somesuch or Marshall or Harlow, after her great grandpapa, or Harrison or Henderson, so many fine names are thoroughly monopolized: Will, for example, William. Willy. Tweedy was not a name at all, but appeared with the bee, still free, at large, at liberty, like Luther, Günter, Stieg, and Gustavo.

"That's it," she said. The busboy scurried away with some dirty dishes. "Run, Gustavo, Run!"

The dessert menu was typed out on a small white card as follows:

Crème Brûlée
Gâteau au Chocolat
Petite Lemon
Black Russian Tort
Pecan Tart
Vanilla Ice Cream, Local Sprig of Mint

"What will it be?" said William as the waiter stood by. "What's good?"

"We have wonderful choices here," said the waiter.

"Oh I love dessert," said Helene, "I just love it."

"Looks wonderful," said Michael.

"What will it be?" said William.

"Anything at all for me," said Tweedy. She set the menu down on a faint old stain.

"Shall we split a few?" asked Helene to the menu.

"Three will be fine," said William, "after a meal like that one."

"That's fine," said Michael. "Three for the four of us."

"Wonderful," said Helene. "I agree completely."

"Tweedy dear?" said William.

"Anything at all," said Tweedy.

"You had better come back," said Helene to the waiter. The waiter went away.

"I always like their chocolate gateau here," said William.

"I say the gateau, it's won awards, the crème brûlée too, and Helene, what do you like the looks of?"

"I'm for the Black Russian," said Michael.

"I think I'm for the Petite Lemon," Helene said.

"Fine, fine," said William. "But we won't need two chocolate cakes. Either the gateau or the Black Russian, but not both. Gateau is my favorite."

"Sounds wonderful to me," said Helene, and waved to the waiter.

"I'm for the Black Russian," Michael said.

"Perhaps the waiter can bring the Black Russian," said Tweedy. "I think we are decided."

"Gateau is better," said William.

"Or the busboy," said Tweedy.

"Don't complicate things, dear," said Helene to Tweedy.

"Gateau," said William to the waiter who had arrived. "And one crème brûlée and the lemon—"

"I'm having the Black Russian," said Michael to the waiter. "I'll have that with extra forks."

"That's four," said William. "We don't need four."

"Can that busboy deliver the desserts?" said Tweedy to the waiter. He nodded, of course.

"My grandfather was from Kiev," said Michael. "I'm settled on the Black Russian."

"But I tell you, the gateau is the specialty here. You are new in town," said William. "I know this place."

"I'm fine with both cakes," said Michael, "two chocolate cakes is fine with me." He winked at Helene and she smiled back. "All of them are fine, I'm not picky."

"Two chocolates is fine with me too," said Helene. "And the crème brûlée."

"Helene, really, see what I'm saying," said William. "Two

chocolates is no fun at all. And what of the lemon you wanted? Keep your backbone, dear, the lemon has several awards too."

"I'm feeling chocolate tonight," she said. "I'm for chocolate and more chocolate."

Tweedy hiccuped at forty-one seconds, progress, progress.

William stood up and walked around the table. He pounded Tweedy three times on the back and returned to his seat. The waiter hovered ten feet off. The other tables were clearing. Empty chairs sprawled in disorder. Helene straightened the centerpiece, a vase shaped like a seal and a girl dancing in white porcelain. A red rose stood up between the partners.

Gustavo was far across the room. He piled himself with dirty plates in the crook of his arm, up the arm to the shoulder, the tray and the other arm, more and more. He slumped under the burden, the heaviest thing she had ever seen. Gustavo saving for college, or to take his girl to the prom, to get a tux and cummerbund to match her dress, blue blue, Gustavo blue, my blue darling. He'll need better nutrition if he's to get his way with her on prom night. Extra body fat. No girl likes a skinny boy. Gustavo tottered under dishes for her. He lifted goblets with smears and platters with blood still pooled with gravy and sprigs of garnish, all for her. All to crush her in the plush of the limo. Tweedy once dreamed so also. She could understand his error: that limo will cost him. How will he possibly get the limo, or equivalent? On his probable wages and meager tips doled out by stingy waiters and cooks? He will also need to tip the driver. The cap and suit are always extra. He must pay extra for the driver to bow to his girl, to open the door for her, to tuck her hem so the door won't crush it. To show the depth of his feeling. The effect of her proximity to his body. To his lungs, diaphragm and extremities. *I'm alive. Can you feel it?* Is what the limo will express. He must pay and pay to lean on the girl on the bumper, hips and shoulders under blue satin, lips smeared pink. She will taste like pear. Poor Gustavo. He'd do better to drive the car himself. Forget the driver. Save the cash. The girl won't mind. They never do. For a good life, a good girl will do anything.

The busboy stacked and stacked dishes. Impossible.

"Everyone needs help," she said. "Everyone needs it sometimes."

No one heard it. They were watching the busboy: the table, the room, the bee. Each with his own view and interpretation of the subject and meaning: He balanced the tray on the flat of his hand and swayed and tottered. He was a pyramid of dishes steering for the kitchen; the waiter gave a wide berth as Gustavo staggered under the weight. He tipped and swiveled at the double doors. Tweedy waited for his crash, his cacophony of china and silver and teacups, the whole world in the air. For once they will stop their chewing and chatter and look at him. A cure for hiccups is a bullet and a gun, a snakebite, a gas can. The people will push their plates away just as the dishes fly up, the first step to becoming shards, broken handles, and slivers of crystal, which will slide twenty feet under the tables, come to rest near a shoe in one second flat: an eternity. He will sweep it all up after, every fragment, while the tables snap-snap for the check and the waiter running: "no dessert for us, thank you, or you or you, no chocolate or lemon." They will all go home. They will all go to bed, stupendous, awaiting destruction still, pale pink and polite.

Gustavo pushed open the double doors with his narrow backside. He twisted himself and the stack around him. He disappeared inside the light of the kitchen.

William slapped the table. "Have what you want then." The waiter stood by.

"I think we need four," said Helene.

"Four is absurd," said William. He slapped the table.

"I want the Black Russian," said Michael to the waiter.

"We know what you want," said William.

"I'm talking to him," said Michael of the waiter. "Black Russian, Black Russian, Black Russian." Gustavo pushed silently through the double doors. His tray was empty again. He stood surveying the tables.

William held his head. Gustavo swept a dollar bill from a table while the waiter was distracted. Tweedy began to clap. "Bravo! Bravo!"

Helene said, "Perhaps the pecan tart."

"My God," said William.

"Art Beeker liked pecan pie," said Michael.

"The man is dead," said William, standing.

"And we will have the chocolate gateau as well," said Helene.

"I won't eat a bite of it," said William. "Not one bite."

"Do as you must," said Helene.

Art Beeker had been a fair card player at the Club and he did not like dessert at all. Tweedy remembered this distinctly. Otherwise, Art was unmemorable, a fading man.

Helene ordered the pecan tart and the scoop of vanilla. The waiter asked Tweedy last, after a hiccup. She said, "I think I'll try the powder room again," and stood and ordered three vanillas with mint as she went. In the powder room Tweedy dug in her turquoise handbag. She wrote the note with lipstick on an envelope. Punctuation and style were simple and the envelope was old, flat and clean from a remote zippered pocket rarely opened. It had been waiting there blind to its future. At the table Tweedy ate the ice cream slowly, never with such pleasure. She tried each of three spoons laid out by her busboy. She drank long drinks of water between. She pulled the ice cream off the spoons to the ends of her lips. They turned white and cold. She could not come close to finishing. She offered to share half-heartedly. She licked her lips and a finger. She hiccuped.

Helene set the car keys by William's plate. Gustavo cleared the plates around them. Then the check came.

"Fifteen percent, no more," William said. "This waiter was only average."

"In Europe a tip's an insult," Michael said. "They'd throw you in the back alley for fifteen percent."

"Twenty is a minimum," said Helene, on and on, so they never saw the handoff from Tweedy to busboy: the tray, the envelope, the lipstick words, and the turquoise keychain, which the busboy stuffed down the front of his pants. He already looked older.

"My spare set," Tweedy whispered. "Follow me. Make it look convincing."

The table was soon cleared.

Soon, in the alley, Gustavo with the envelope stood smoking. He was not usually one to smoke, but he puffed. The brick was hard on his shoulder. Busboy was only his first career. He read the lipstick words again.

"Take the Car . . . ," said the envelope.

He watched the party of four under the awning, which was blue and white with lights on the skirting. The party parted, one couple walking one way and the other the other. Gustavo puffed. The chill shivered his skin, how surprising after the ovens and candles, the night of sweat and running. Michael and Helene stood beside the parking meter. They pecked, then Helene clicked away down the street.

". . . Take the Girl," the envelope continued.

Gustavo watched William find his keys and slip one in the door of the long creamy car in front of the deli. William opened the door for Tweedy then walked around the car and dropped into it. The car pulled out. The headlights slashed the bumpers and tires parked along the street and the glass in the storefronts. Gustavo rubbed the stub out on brick. Gustavo threw the stub on the dirt where it smoked long after he'd slipped in behind the wheel of his old Dodge Dart parked in the alley and followed the long creamy car.

The car made a few stops on the way home. The Dart pulled over and waited. Gustavo was not usually the type for rereading, for following strangers, for waiting outside on curbs and lighting another, but there was pleasure in all this new. He reread the envelope. All of it.

"Take the Car. Take the Girl. For a Good Life if you can," it said.

At the liquor store William walked in then walked out with a bag. At the drugstore Tweedy walked in. A horse and buggy trotted past from the Bavarian Hotel on the corner. Gustavo had seen these horses hundreds of times but had never seen the mist made with their noses. How the buggy driver tapped their swaying hips with the crop, which was small and thin, just for show with horses so well-trained and obedient. Tweedy walked out of the drugstore with a bag. She stood under the awning. She watched the horses and listened to the clop of their shoes. When she saw the Dart across the street, she waved. The long creamy car pulled out and the Dart followed it.

Their home was seven turns away and had brick pillars in front and a hedge. The car turned in. No dogs came running, a good sign. The door opened to the light and then the door shut and the light went out. The Dart parked behind the hedge by the last pillar. Gustavo shuffled papers in his glove box, then the Dart pulled away.

Rivers are convincing in movies, he knew. Gustavo drove to the river. He took the frontage road that was tilted and ridged. He parked the Dart on the river's edge next to old bridge pilings. The front tire rolled in and submerged. His shoes got wet climbing out.

The new bridge was lit up upstream. The headlights passed across and back. They lit up the river waves, the dots and dashes. He unscrewed the license plates with a screwdriver from the tool kit in the trunk.

"OK," he said.

He found a triangle of glass in the sand, since sand and glass are convincing too as are blood and skin. He jabbed his arm with the glass in a hairless muscle, but the blood was meager. He cut over his eyebrow in the rearview mirror for more, a thin clean line, always a gusher according to movies and slap shots on the hockey pond as a boy when winter and blood were as entirely real as gangsters, as hurricanes, as gold and silver mines at the end of caves and no girls at all.

Fresh blood in the eye. He smeared the driver's seat with it, a credible crime scene. He had always wanted one. And blood on the inside of the door, which they would dust for prints, and the steering wheel, which his ex-girlfriend would cry over if they even let her through the cordoned area. Most likely not. She was not immediate family. She'd been such a bitch at prom. That chess team captain with the big teeth. Envelopes need not be obeyed to the letter. One must use judgment, exercise freedom. He wiped his face on his sleeve. They would never look for him.

Gustavo scuffled with himself in the sand. From the marks the police would call it "an unsolved mugging". He bashed the perfect old hood with a head-sized stone for extra credibility. He was sorry for the Dart, his grandmama's, which refused reverse and always would now. He stuffed his tips in his pocket. He threw the wallet with the license in the driver's seat, then rolled up the windows. He pushed the Dart further into the river, which was heavy and pushy. The waves sloshed over the windshield. He threw the triangle glass and stone in the river. The splashes disappeared. He walked out as far as he dared. He cleaned himself of the busboy.

Gustavo lifted the tool kit from the trunk. A Christmas gift from his father. He had really never used the tool kit, never held each tool in his hand and thought of potentials of wrenches and blades. He lifted out the gas can, water jug, and the little suitcase he always kept ready in case of sudden opportunity. He stopped to think. Mistakes are so easy and well-disguised. He leaned on the trunk. At critical times especially. He put the license plates in the little suitcase. He sat in the sand and stones and watched the cars on the new bridge. He listened to the water flow past him toward bigger rivers.

The little suitcase had a handle and wheels. He rolled it over the sand until he noticed the tracks the wheels were making. He carried the suitcase the rest of the way to the frontage road pavement, then went back to wipe the tracks away with his coat. He would wash the coat somewhere new, in some big-mouthed machine with washing instructions in a foreign language. He rolled the suitcase on the frontage road. He carried it when cutting through yards and parks. It was not heavy at all. The coat was tied around his waist. The neighborhood dogs barked on the end of their chains, collars tightening around the necks, as he slid past their backyards and back porches. His feet hurt.

At the car, he dug in his briefs for her turquoise keychain. The key turned in the lock like lemon meringue. He slid across the long creamy seat. He checked the glove box, which contained a man's wallet filled with bills, some cookies in foil (cream custard-filled and ginger thins), and some assorted jewelry. He let the car roll backward. The driveway had just enough downward slope, not too fast or slow. His foot swung out the open door. His foot pushed the asphalt out to sea. His fingers crushed the envelope. He steered with his elbow. It was a heavy car, full of gas, and rolled well. It would sell for a bundle: Texas or Mexico. The Panama Canal. The moon was white. The car backed into the darkened street.

Everyone was sleeping.

No one to thank.

He unwrapped the foil. He wiped his mouth on his damp sleeve, swept the crumbs out the open door, pushed the car down the street, one hand on the wheel and one on the door frame, careful of the hinges, slow and peaceful under big heavy trees. He thanked the branches and leaves lit in elegant street lamps. He gave a thumbs-up to them.

At a safe distance, past the pillars and hedges, he pulled the door shut. The engine started like a maiden voyage. The headlights were excellent. The car was warm and comfortable, smelled nice like the powder room, and was big enough to sleep in.

Canada. Bolivia.

"OK. OK."

He screwed on his old plates at an abandoned farm stand. He crunched last year's kernels underfoot, soggy from recent heavy rains, sprouting pale thin legs in mud. He changed to high tops. He kicked a dried apple in the ditch. He set the envelope on the dash. He was not usually one for maps, for lines on paper claiming to lead somewhere.

The car pulled out south and ran well over the county line.

The Amazing Discovery and Natural History of Carlsbad Caverns

That was Mike hanging on the brass chandelier. He was Tarzan with a crew cut and farm boy grin, swinging upside down. Hilarious. Mel could get Mike to do anything.

The women were laughing their heads off at Mike, mostly South of the Border girls, in their reds, blues, and pinks. They pointed pretty painted fingers up at him. Smiled with big teeth and red lips. The men were laughing their heads off too, clean, starched, tall and white, taller by a head than the local girls. The men were shipped in from their Chicagos, Maines, and Pasadenas to Fort Bliss to be trained up and ready, waiting to ship out.

It was too tight and warm in the Bombardier. The men dabbed their brows with handkerchiefs someone had stitched for them on some back porch. Those who had mislaid their hankies wiped sweat with the back of bare thick arms, or the tail of a damp shirt, or licked the upper lip and swallowed with a chaser. Hot as Hades sure, but if a big black hand had flown in from downtown Hong Kong or Taiwan or Ching Chong to pry at the rafters with black hairy fingers, had pulled off the roof purlin by purlin, had let in some air, then things might have been different.

Mike poured beer on the crowd. The crowd laughed and twirled. Mike twirled his trousers like a lasso. Mel blew a kiss at Mike and handed him up another, which Mike poured on the crowd, which laughed more and leaned and so on. It was a wonderful night. Mike's chandelier will hang there for three decades more, until the Bombardier burns down. The girls will marry and have children by other men than these, and one of the children's children will fly to Mars on the first manned mission. At the launch, this grandmother, stone-blind by then, in her lilac suit, rose in hair, Bible in hand as the rocket glides out of earshot, will picture this night perfectly. Will sit down on the bleachers and rub her neck.

Mel was from McAllen, so was used to the heat. A boy was walking in the crowd with a pretty pistol on a yellow velvet pillow and was talking *español*. He wore a sombrero. The pistol grip was mother-of-pearl, a beauty, made for a female or a duel, someone said. Mel ended up with the sombrero too.

Someone called, "Enough hanky-panky. Let's get back to Base."

Someone else yelled, "Reveille's at six." One man whistled at his pals and the pals herded up. They laughed at something someone said. Mike swung down with one arm. He scratched his armpit and howled.

"What a card," someone said as the men moved to the street. They rubbed their arms in the chill. The Border was like that, hot after dark until it was suddenly cold. Someone called a cab.

In the street, Mike hopped into his pants. He zipped up, "Where's my goddamn belt?" But the belt was gone forever, kicked under the bar by a girl's pink heel, never to be discovered by anyone ever, although a long-handled broom will almost grab it next Easter. The belt will burn up, even the brass buckle, with the rest of the Bombardier in the Heroes Day Fire that will take the whole block to the river.

For now, Mike bunched his pants with one hand. He stood on the curb and cracked the seal of a bottle and drank. The sombrero was huge on Mel's head and Mike said, "I like that hat. I sure do like it."

Others agreed, nodded. Time passed, a few minutes, a quarter hour, a cab came and took some men, another cab came, so on.

The sombrero had red balls around the rim like a toy. They swung in unison and glowed when any car drove by.

"Let me try it," said Mike.

"Get back," said Mel, and he slapped his friend's hand, but nice. The sombrero looked like a crown in the headlights. The city was dim and the dwindled crowd smoked on the street. Nearby the river flowed dry and someone said, "Does it ever rain?"

"Godforsaken desert," said someone else.

The rooftops were flat and poor. Flags and clouds strayed in the small breeze and drooped. The moon was up but hidden. It haloed the corniced peak of El Banco. The men leaned on brick and saluted with bottles when three jets roared over, banked, then disappeared north to home and hangar.

"Let me try it on," said Mike.

"You always want what I got," said Mel, but he let Mike try the hat. The crowd laughed at Mike. They passed a bottle, then Mike set the hat back on Mel's head. Happiness is so small a thing, and they had it on the street for a while, just like that, happiness. Mike stumbled into Mel, who had grabbed a girl in an orange dress who had just come out the door. They all three swayed together for a turn, like waltzing, until Mel shoved the girl to an electric pole for a kiss. Her arms went crazy. She screeched like a cat and the sombrero fell.

"My nose!" said Mel. She'd made a direct hit to the bridge of it. "Son of a bitch!" said Mel with his face to the wall, his hands were up like praying since his nose was bleeding like crazy.

The girl went running and it was Mike who made chase. "I'll get her," Mike said, clutching his pants, but she was faster than one might guess. The crowd was excited. Mel watched between bloody fingers and they hooted and whistled at her big bottom swinging. "Will you listen to those shoes," someone said. "Like hooves clomping, clickity, click clack!" someone said. The girl hurdled a small fallen tree.

When a cab turned the corner, Mel whistled and Mike ran back.

"My dad would have a cow over that tree," said Mike trotting up.

"I'll see that cow in the future," said Mel to the corner where the girl in the orange dress had turned. Mel and Mike slid in the backseat of the cab, Mike behind the cabbie. The nameplate on the dash said "Richard" but with no picture. It was any ordinary cab.

"To Fort Bliss, amigo," said Mike to the cabbie. "*Mucho dinero* for you."

"Don't you have any heat in this rig?" said Mel. "I'm freezing." He adjusted the sombrero, which blocked the rearview when he tipped his head. He licked blood from his lip. His nose was turning blue and swelling.

"Heat's busted," said the cabbie, then the cab pulled from the curb and sped north.

"My dad will be milking soon," said Mike. The street was closing up. Men and girls walked in couples and threes. "My mother's a poor milker."

"Who'd want to milk a cow?" said Mel.

"It's more pleasant than you'd think," said Mike. "Restful and gives you time for thinking."

"Who'd want to milk a cow?" said Mel. He dabbed his nose on his cuff.

"You OK?" asked the cabbie. "You need a hospital? I can take you there."

"My friend had a run in with a she-wolf," said Mike.

"A rabid bovine," said Mel.

"Looks more like Joe Louis got him," said the cabbie. "Or my mother-in-law."

"Ha ha ha, a joker," said Mike. "Mel, how do you like this guy?" He smacked the cabbie's shoulder. He drank from the bottle, and drank again.

"Take a left," Mel said.

The cab swerved around the fallen tree and turned. A block up, the girl in the orange dress stood under an awning, bent over, hands on her face.

"Slow down," said Mel, and the cab slowed. Mike jumped out of the cab still rolling. "I'll take care of this." The girl sprinted down an alley and Mike did too. They disappeared at the end of it.

The cab waited in the street. The station played a mariachi, which finished with a flourish of trumpets. The announcer said, "Tomorrow will be hot," and another song started, a waltz. Awnings leaned down and fire escapes wound up, dark and peaceful. Steps dropped away. Another cab rolled near. The drivers signed to each other and the high beams flashed. The other cab was green, unusual for the area, a new model. The green cab will pass on, will be crushed in a head-on the day Kennedy is shot over in Dallas, so neither the bloody car wreck nor the funerals will be much noted in the papers: invisible, inconsequential.

The green cab passed on. It was any dark street again.

"Who's that girl?" said the cabbie. "Why's he chasing that girl?"

"She's no one," said Mel. "Some bitch. Mike takes care of things for me." Mel swigged and blood from his nose smeared on the neck of the bottle. "Maybe I know that girl," said the cabbie. "We live near here."

"You don't know her," said Mel.

There was a brass frame hanging from the rearview mirror. "These are my kids in here," said the cabbie and touched the frame. "Richie, Consuelo, Kiki, and Gloria, the baby. I tell them stories sometimes to make them sleep. Like King Arthur and Lancelot, or General Grant, Alexander or Abraham Lincoln. Big stories and how they should live in the future."

"How should they live in the future?" said Mel.

"How to be good men and girls," said the cabbie.

"Then all your kids will be good little men and girls."

"I tell them all about the desert sometimes too. I have ten books about this desert and the mountains and caves in it. We have the most stupendous caves out there in our desert."

"Well, fine," said Mel. He shifted the sombrero and drank.

"I have three books on it in the trunk," said the cabbie.

"That's just swell," said Mel. "A regular rolling library."

It was a dark street at that hour. The cabbie looked down the alley. "He won't hurt her," said the cabbie.

"Only if she deserves it," said Mel. "Only in that case." The headlights beamed down the street in two cones of light that flicked from high beams to low beams with the cabbie's finger. High low, high low, and the street shifted and moved: the brick walls rose and fell, the trash bins were boulders, then sawed down trees, then trash bins, and so on. Holes and doorways blinked like hungry things.

"Might as well shut her down," said Mel. "Cut the lights." The sombrero dipped down over his face the old fashioned way, like napping at high noon in some pueblo. But the cabbie did not shut down the engine or lights. The cabbie watched the empty alley. The red balls on the rim were now black. Mel tipped his head, breathed blood back in, and the balls tipped up like the ride at the June fair. The kids would love that ride, the Ferris wheel, wave down from the top. The cabbie twisted the radio dial. The yellow cab hummed. A curtain pulled shut up in a second story window. The shadow of a stray dog darted out and back into shadow. They waited for Mike. A slow song sang with a chocolate voice.

There once lived a cowboy named Jim White. He's known and famous across the globe as the discoverer of the world's most colossal, most beautiful, most spectacular, most stupendous, and all-around best caves. Now, these caves he found happen to be right here in our very own desert. On a clear day you can look out that window and see the mountains they're in. The caves are eight hundred feet down, a maze of three hundred caves at least, gigantic bubbles in the solid rock. A few are big enough to fit a town. Jim found the entrance to the caves one day while herding calves: a tunnel two hundred feet down—the blackest hole you ever saw.

What did Jim do when he found the blackest hole you ever saw? Did he say, "I'm tired. I think I'll go back to the ranch for a nap"? Or, "Well behold, there's a mighty big and interesting hole in the ground right there, but I have no ladder to reach it with"? Did he say, "Some other man can explore that hole, for I have no expertise"? No, Jim didn't say any of that. He went and built a ladder two hundred feet tall.

Then he climbed right down in the hole on his new ladder, then three miles down the sloping tunnel, like plumbing the belly of an immense stone snake. Sometimes Jim crawled on hands and knees. He had no friend with him and only the small glow of his lamp to see by. His reward was the biggest cave anyone's ever seen, that's a man for you. Later, Jim brought a boy with him, a Mexican, a pony-tender and ranch hand, since the other cowboys were too scared to come. But Jim mostly explored the caves alone. He plumbed pits with no bottom and wandered chambers with no ceiling. He saw sights too strange and marvelous to speak of.

That was 1901, more than fifty years ago. Sure, other cowboys had seen the big hole in the ground in their wanderings, but none bothered to look into it further. The Indians of this desert must have known, since they make every root and rock their business. But it is well known that Indians are deadly afraid of the dark. Who else knew the caves? Not the bees nor the birds, though they surely swooped down for a peek at the tunnel's mouth when the sun angled right. The bats knew, they lived in the caves, of course, as did the fishes swimming down in the cold black pools. But the bats and fishes are purblind creatures. What does knowing mean for such as them? The bat hears the stone and flies. The fish feels water and swims. It goes to show one thing sure: the greatest grandest things on earth are nothing at all until some man comes along, points it out, and says: "Hey lookie here!"

Jim White never looked for fame and fortune. He appeared any regular man. He was born on a ranch no one's heard of and was riding the range before he turned eight. His horse was his best pal. He wore a sombrero since it served him best. He was a freckled man since birth, a gringo, but good anyway, his heart was clean. Jim ate rice and beans with any man, and beef when there was some. He liked cattle and cactus, firesides, and tall tales with happy endings. He was poor with writing but managed a letter to Mother once a week her life through. Nor was he one for praying or dreaming up what God might carve if He set His hands to limestone. But once such sights invade a cowboy's small parched brain, they cannot be rooted out except by death or terrible infirmity.

Sleep now, my darling children.

Another waltz played on the station. A light flickered on in a high window down the street, then off. Mike trotted from down the alley. He slid in the cab, slammed the back door, and smiled. "Drive on, Ricardo."

"Who's that girl?" said the cabbie to Mike.

In a few blocks Mike said to Mel, "That nose is a geyser."

The cab drove past the theater with the marquee lights out. At the cathedral a cat sat at the crack in the big doors. "I got married there," the cabbie said, and pointed at the doors. "Funerals, baptisms. Everything is there." The bell tower reached up, but no one looked. "I got married there right before they shipped me to France. My wife, she worries about everything. You boys married?"

"What outfit?" said Mike.

"The 4th infantry," said the cabbie. "Where you boys from?"

"Omaha Beach?" said Mike.

"Utah Beach."

"Utah Beach my ass," said Mel. "Damn it's cold."

"My dad was in France in the First War," said Mike. "I'd give my eye teeth for Utah Beach." The houses were snug on the street like a tribe, low and dark behind stone walls: a pile of rocks, a pile of sand, a pile of tires covered with sand and rocks and glass in splinters and shards. Mike said, "They say the Channel was red a mile out to sea."

"I couldn't say the color of the water," said the cabbie.

"They say it was a bridge of legs and backs," said Mike. "You a fair swimmer?"

"I swam to shore. I got this scar." The cabbie showed the side of his neck under the stiff collar. "My wife, she had our first while I was gone."

"That's something," said Mike. "That neck is really something. What I wouldn't give."

"My youngest just lost her front tooth. Now my oldest kid's teeth need fixing. Time flies." The cabbie rubbed his fingers together like money. Mike and Mel passed the bottle between them. Blood from the neck smeared Mike's hands and cuffs. Mike offered the bottle to the cabbie, who shook his head, and Mike and Mel drank again. The dash glowed green and the town thinned. The cab rolled up a low hill.

"He could have nicked his neck shaving," said Mel to Mike. "There's a thousand ways to nick a neck." The cab crested the hill. The river lay far below, just a black line.

"Does it ever flood?" said Mike.

"It floods," said the cabbie. "It runs a thousand miles at least."

Mountains busted out ragged and parched from place to place and the cab rolled down the north side. Mel looked at the soft place behind the cabbie's ear, "He could have read up on Utah Beach in any book."

"You hear that, Ricardo?" said Mike. "Mel says you read up on Utah Beach in a book."

"Sure. I read it in a book. I was never in Normandy, never

saw Paris, my barber nicked my neck a good one, better tell my wife where I was all that time. You boys are smart as whips."

"Don't let Mel get your goat," said Mike.

"Sure," said the cabbie.

"That nose needs ice."

"Sure," said the cabbie.

Mel pressed his nose to his collar.

"How many kids you got?" said Mike.

"Two boys and two girls."

"And some's got crooked teeth," said Mel. "A shame."

"People hate people with crooked teeth," said Mike. "It's a sad fact of nature."

"My girl tripped on the foot of the table, the tooth came right out," said the cabbie. "Of course there was blood, any girl would have cried. I found the tooth, cleaned it. The roots of a baby's tooth are exactly like a screw. You know that? I never did. So I set that tooth back in her head like new. Didn't know if I could, it was just last week."

Mel said, "Crooked teeth, crooked soul." He drank.

The land rose again, fell again, rose again. The dogs barked from chain to chain in the yards behind the walls, barked from house to house. Now the last house, the last parked car, the last liquor store with lights out, the sign that said, "Come back soon, y'all." The edge of the desert. The sombrero tipped up against the back glass and blotted the town. The music played out strong and joyful till miles of sand killed the trumpets.

Jim White did not just stumble onto his caves by chance. He was invited in. Here's how:

From a distance he had thought it was a volcanic eruption. Or the end of the world. The calves he'd been driving agreed, fled to high ground at the sight of black swirling spew. Jim's horse shied and bucked too, refused to go closer. But he was the very best sort of horse, and Jim tied his shirt across the horse's eyes and roped him to a bush, which soothed him. Jim crawled on hands and knees to the edge of the hole where the cloud poured forth.

Millions and millions of bats. The bats swarmed and banked around him. They fanned his face with ten million soft wings. The bats tipped and turned around the sombrero and the sombrero fell and they banked around it. They squeaked and chattered, the echo doubled them, so pretty a sound it was! They made Jim weak and strong at the exact same time. "There's no end to these bats," he thought, but still he waited because there's an end to all things, a cowboy learns this much. When the bats were done and gone, the hole they left was black as a solid wall. Jim dropped a stone down and listened. Stones and hours dropped and the day passed. The calves, lonely, came back and stood with the horse and they all chewed weeds. Jim built a fire. He flung down a flaming arm of cactus that arced and landed far below. It burned as bright as it could, but, in all that dark, barely gave a hint of the width of the bats' vast doorway. Jim never saw the hat again.

That night at the bunkhouse, Jim talked of cows and branding and listened to cowboy jokes. He let his horse lick the plate clean, as always, then bunked in. But how could he sleep? Next day, Jim gathered an ax, some wire, and a bit of rope. He filled the kerosene lamp to overflowing, packed his kit and departed on his horse, looking out for likely trees along the way. He'd need many to build his ladder.

Once, later on, when he'd been up and down the ladder so many times that the bats were pals to him, Jim found a dead man in the caves. A skeleton sleeping in a crotch of rock. The size of him was twice as big as any man Jim had ever seen, though the skull was exactly normal. At first sight, Jim thought he'd found some breed of giants, Red Men from the Plain who lived in the caves, then died. But when Jim touched the big man's arm, every bone crumbled to dust. Every bone but the skull. Scientists later explained the chemistry: limestone and water dripping, bloating the bones.

Jim carried the skull out of the cave like a treasure. He lent it to a doctor in Carlsbad, who lent it to a doctor in Cloudcroft, who lent it to a doctor in Weed. In this way, the skull was lost. That skull would have been the prize of Jim's famous cave museum.

The road outside town was a two-lane and smooth. It was built for buggies with spokes and horses, long before Fort Bliss, then improved. The road aimed at the spot where three searchlights swiveled together, green, red, and green. Dizzy and earnest. The cab buzzed north between the spines of mountains. Birds blew up across the headlights from time to time, but ten thousand others crouched in weeds. Dust devils eddied, spun up, and disappeared unseen. A snake S'd off the concrete at the cab's first vibrations and was long gone before the cab whizzed past, disappearing with her fifty thousand twins. The sand spat at the glass, a trillion trillion grains per fistful, blinding the cab and shoving it across the road. The moon slit the sky, it silvered the mountains and cactus which stood in disordered salute to the road.

Mel said, "I'm not tired in the least. I could drive out all night."

The framed picture swung from the rearview mirror, smooth like a pendulum. The cabbie's finger stilled the frame: Kiki in front, holding Gloria in his lap, they grinned out at their father with Connie behind; the tall sister was turned to Richie, who was taller, saying something to him just as the shutter opened. The cabbie let the frame swing free. He tried the radio again but the static sounded like sand and he twisted it off. He rolled down the window, sand blew in. He rolled the window up.

"They'd string us up as AWOL if we drove out all night," said Mike. "I can take or leave desert."

The cab flew on like a bee.

"Reveille's at six," said Mike. He leaned up. "It must be coming on four. I want some shuteye. What time is it?" If there was a clock on the front dash it was dead. The other dials glowed green in the cabbie's face. The speedometer needle shivered as the cab sped on at 66 miles per hour. The gas was below half, plenty for an up and back to Base. The box for heat was at the cabbie's brown-creased knee. It was cold. Mike sang:

> *Daisy, Daisy give me your answer do.*
> *I'm half crazy over the love of you.*
> *It won't be a stylish marriage. I can't afford a carriage.*
> *But you'll look sweet, upon the seat, of a bicycle built for two.*

"Shut that clap trap," said Mel.

"You shut it, Mel, I like that tune. What time is it?" He drank. "Reveille's at six."

"Sing it on your wedding day," said Mel. "You like that song, Ricardo?'

"This desert, way back, was an inland sea," said the

cabbie. "Was once completely underwater. I know all about this desert."

"Open your eyes," said Mel, who licked his lips. His nose was dry but the smell of blood had lingered for miles. "Open your goddamn eyes."

"Those mountains behind Base, they're old coral reefs built up by clams, urchins, and such. Think of how many urchins. There's caves in the ground famous the world over. Big enough to fit a town." The cabbie's fingers found the switch for heat and he flicked it on and off. The needle hovered over 68 miles per hour.

"Last month I found a starfish by the latrine," said Mike. "I sent it home to my folks."

"They're the most beautiful caves you ever saw, gold and pearl swirled in the rock. They were made after the sea dried up. I tell my kids, 'Squint your eyes. A giant squid is at our heels! Whales and sharks is winding around like one of Ike's submarines, peaceful like lambs, eels and fishes missiling around, jellyfish, pink, orange, and green, waving their arms and legs, that would be fine.' I say, 'Wouldn't it be fine?'"

"You got kids?" said Mike. "I'd like some kids."

"Give me that bottle," said Mel. He pressed his swollen cheek against the cold window. The sombrero was flattened by the glass. The glass was smeared with blood and sweat.

"I got four kids," said the cabbie. "I know all the cave stories by heart. They say, 'Papa, tell again about the caves and the bats and the big man!' and I say, 'Alright then, I'll tell it again when your heads are on the pillows.'"

"I don't care for caves," said Mel and looked at his watch, which was too dark to see. "It's cold. Let's get some heat." The cabbie flicked the switch on and off.

"This certainly explains the starfish," said Mike.

"Your starfish makes a hill of beans," said Mel and drank. "What does he know? Nothing." A mile passed. The Base was a halo sprawled low behind the searchlights. "I could use some heat."

"The heat's been busted for a week," said the cabbie. A mile passed. The speedometer needle reached 72 then passed it, onward to 75 miles per hour. "Was that girl OK?" said the cabbie. "I've got two little girls myself."

"It's a simple question of justice," said Mike. "Try the heat again."

"God damn it," said Mel. "There's no heat. Ricardo already said."

The cabbie tried the switch again and the heat came on, blasted warm for a mile, then shut off again. "God damn it," said Mel.

"What's eating you?" said Mike. Another mile passed by, cactus waved in the cool wet blue. "My dad lost a finger in France. I do also know that. There's many things I know."

"He could have lost it chopping cabbage," said Mel.

"But he didn't lose it chopping cabbage," said Mike.

"What do you know about chopped-off fingers?" said Mel. "Were you there when he chopped off his goddamn finger? Did you see the blood? What do you know? What do I know, what does he know about anything: seas, deserts, girls, or mermaids. Hills of beans, mountains of beans, that's all."

Mike drank, Mel drank. The bottle sloshed. A mile passed. The searchlights fanned the stars. The brown mountains to the north disappeared behind the growing searchlights. A jet could spot Base from one hundred miles with those searchlights waving and dancing, green, red, green: "Come here, this way, come here to land." The needle swung right, 84, 85 miles per hour, leaned into 86 and quivered there.

"Faster," said Mike.

"It's fast," said the cabbie and Mike kicked the seat and the cabbie jumped.

"Faster," said Mike.

The foot quivered on the pedal. The legs in regular brown pants quivered. Fear enters through the ears, eyes, and nose, any orifice, but accumulates and settles itself in the limbs and extremities: 87 miles per hour can seem slow to some. Consider the jet that will fly over soon and land without incident on the runway beyond the gatehouse. The pilot will sleep all morning, take a shower at noon, and lose his father's wristwatch in the mess. He will ship out without finding it. They will crash on the transport to the Theater: over the Pole, a goose in the engine and a glacier receding at one inch per year.

"I know I was born too," said Mike. "I know plenty. I was born. Here I am. You were born. And he was born." Mike pointed the bottle at the cabbie. "There's a moon up there, I can see it, way out far. Someone will fly there sometime, pitch a tent and eat cheese."

"Ha ha ha," laughed Mel.

Forty-four seconds passed, a fast mile, the needle at 89. The cabbie's knuckles and wrists were green.

"Sure you were born, yes, but who's your daddy?" said Mel, sitting up like he was having fun.

"You need religion thinking that," said Mike.

"Luckily, you and your friend Ricardo here are in the exact same boat," said Mel. "You can grieve your women troubles together."

"He's not my friend," said Mike.

"Your pop was a long time in France. Ricardo was a long time away at Utah Beach," said Mel. "Things can get very lonely back at the casa?"

"Utah Beach is something else altogether," said Mike.

"Women are frail," said Mel.

"I'm the spitting image of my pop," said Mike. "I got that picture by my bunk."

"You got an uncle?" said Mel. "I bet you're the spitting image of your uncle too."

"My uncle lives in Milwaukee," said Mike.

"So many cows to be milked," said Mel. "The truck needs tending. A man is needed for many things."

"Why you son of a bitch!" yelled Mike, and in the back-seat arms and legs kicked and swung and thumped the doors and seat. The grunting and groaning was in earnest at first, then Mel yelled, "Goddamn, lighten up!" When the pistol flashed and cracked, the laughing only got louder, "Crazy son of a bitch, ha ha ha!" A new wind screamed through the fresh hole in the roof.

The cab slowed to 22, tried to sway to the shoulder, but Mel said, "Keep going," and the cab drove on. His son Richie had black hair and black eyes. Consuelo, black hair black eyes, Kiki, black black same. Gloria, round and brown and a new front tooth, Gloria Gloria, the children often lifted their heads in the night, turned their pillows without waking at all, a miracle of unconsciousness.

"We could be dead in a month anyway," Mel said. "Face down in tree roots we can't even pronounce the name of, Ping-Pong Bing-Bong, eh, Ricardo? We ship out in a week."

"You're a sourpuss sometimes," said Mike. "You can really ruin my fun."

"We'll be laying there in the mud. A pack of squint-eyed

little yellow men will sneak up quiet behind, quick and nimble through the jungle leaves, and put a pistol to your soft baby temple. Right there." Mel tapped the cabbie's temple with his pinkie finger. The cabbie jerked his head away. The needle got blurry at 91. The sand was blue, the black sky was getting blue in the east.

"I heard that's so, quick little squint-eyed yellow men by the millions," Mike said and drank. "I'd like to shoot something tonight."

Mel said, "If he doesn't shoot you on the spot in the mud, he'll take you back to his hole in the ground and tie your hands. Bind your eyes. Spin you round and laugh his yellow head off before he shoots you, or guts you, or worse."

"What could be worse than gutting?"

"There's plenty worse. These squint-eyes have been at it five thousand years. It's an art form they practice."

"I wouldn't let him," said Mike. "I'd kill him first."

"How'd you kill him first?" said Mel. "He's got you at gunpoint."

"I'd have my knife. It's tucked in my boot and I'll slit his yellow belly up the middle like a calf."

"That might do it," said Mel. "Now you're thinking."

"Pull his insides out and leave them for the dogs," said Mike.

"And the birds," Mel said. "Picking each last bit of him. Swallowing some and bringing the rest home to the hungry mouths at the nest."

"I hate him, that's what," said Mike. Five deer in a set leapt all together along the right shoulder, dashed across in the headlights, and stopped in a set on the left shoulder. "Quick give me that pistol," and Mike. "I'll get some practice right now." He rolled down the window and shot three times.

"Don't use them up!" said Mel. "We might need them." He tried to snatch the pistol, but Mike held it up and away. "Suit yourself," said Mel.

"I think I got one," said Mike.

"Those deer will live to be sixty-two," said Mel. "You've gotten nothing tonight."

The cabbie took the brass picture frame from the mirror and slid it in his pocket. His hand stayed in the pocket for a mile, then two miles. The searchlight swung greater and greater, taking everything up, taking the whole sky. The gatehouse to Fort Bliss shone as a small gold gleam on a hill. Miles passed quickly. The gatehouse grew bigger and brighter, a yellow seed, a kernel. "I love this night," said Mel. "I vote for driving out as far as we can go."

"Tarred and feathered," said Mike, and yawned. He rolled down the window, spit, rolled up, yawned again. He sniffed the barrel of the pistol. "Solitary confinement. Scrubbing the latrine for AWOL. I'm tired."

"We can hunt down some dolphins and squid. Mark down every variety of sand. I say let's drive out."

"Reveille's at six. We can't goddamn drive out."

"Of course we can drive out," said Mel. "Ricardo will drive us out. We are free men, aren't we?"

The cabbie sweated in the chill. His hands on the wheel were slender hands, like a piano player's hands or a girl's. 95 miles per hour bent the needle into copper green . . . 96 . . . 97 . . . 98.6 . . . a brain will cook at 108°F, but this chassis was built for speed: 180 miles per hour at the end of the green dial where the needle could lie down and rest some.

"My dad's into the chickens by now. Chickens were always my job. I bet the tractor's cranky." Mike yawned again.

"He'll hire a hand," said Mel.

"A hand's not the same," said Mike. "He's old."

The cab rocketed toward Base. The gatehouse gleam grew on a hill, and in every direction nothing but sand.

Across those mountains there is no dirt or clay in the ground, no forest, no fields. The earth is a ball of sand to the middle, and heavy. There are no cities with cobblestone or brick or cement cracking. There is no rain, since the sky is sand, no pond or puddle, sand cliffs drop to sand seas. This is no lake with vines and fishes, no river with trees on the banks that from time to time plunge into the stream to be washed down three thousand miles until snagged on the bottom, the roots looped in the roots of some other tree that fell fifty or five hundred years before. The two will never harpoon the bellies of small frail crafts, never tangled and linked in mud, never rotting as one, since there is no such thing as mud. Nor is there a boat in the desert, of course. No oak anywhere to build one, iron for an anchor. No house with a sink and soap, no bed with a wife who wakes at the sniffle leaning in the doorway. Here are only lizards and beetles, sand and aboriginal thinking.

The cabbie wiped his brow on his sleeve.

"I love this night," said Mel. "It's our desert tonight."

The gatehouse two miles ahead is an A-frame. The A-frame has a black-and-white gate next to it. The black-and-white gate swings up and down by way of a crank. A man stands by the crank. The cab will turn slow to the gatehouse, like a Sunday drive. The blinker ticking right, right, right.

"I was born for this desert," said Mel. "I vote for driving out."

"My wife'll be worried if I don't get back," said the cabbie. "Be calling everyone looking for me, like all get out."

"My mother's a real worrier too," said Mike. "I vote for turning in."

The cab hugged the right shoulder, Our Father who art in Heaven. One mile yet to the gatehouse and the gleam of that gatehouse was strong, "Come this way." Thy Kingdom come Thy will be done, the cab sped on. The cactus everywhere were the low, many-armed breed with spiked hands. They did not tremble.

An A-frame, a good solid A-frame. The soldier at the gatehouse will lean at the window, while the searchlights wave behind him like wings. He'll say, "I hope you boys had a fine time so late. You'll suffer for it come reveille." He'll smile as he says it, a kind man, a forgiving man, deliver us, please deliver us, just a boy really, his cheeks pink from sunburn and coldburn, any trace of pigment in this Viking soldier's skin was from some slave girl from Greenland or Nova Scotia, some kind of trespass in the belly of the ship. The ship had floated east and procreated. The soldier at the gatehouse will crank up the gate and the gate will rise. It will rise up and the cab will roll on, deliver them through.

The caves are a constant 52 degrees. Jim's mother never saw his caves, since she was not one for the underground. She lived her whole life on floorboards. When Jim's mother lay dying, Jim left the caves to see her off. "Jim, my dear son," she'd said, "I want to look fine for my Maker, but this hair of mine is a real shame." The very next day Jim loaded his mother in his cart. He hitched his horse and toted her across the river to a beauty parlor of repute. She prayed on the way, out loud so passers could hear it. They bowed their heads too, the gravity of it. People stepped clear as he carried her in. Jim lay her head in the sink and the cowboy washed the hair now gray forever and ever, Amen. Once Jim wrote of the caves, "Mother, the columns hoist the ceiling like Hercules! They are twisted and vined like a giant's arm, so big as to make the tallest redwood look puny! As for bats, it's true their faces are ugly to look at, but the bats do keep your son from getting lonely. I wish you could see them fly like angels through my silver stone forest, for surely it is the nearest to Heaven on Earth, Glory be! Gloria Gloria and Hallelujah too!"

"She'll be waking soon," said the cabbie. "My wife will send men looking."

"A worrier wears a man down, don't she just?" said Mike. "With my mother, it's chickens first and foremost. Then what's leached in the well: arsenic, lead, polio, scarlet fever. Lice and the sheets need changing and if the cans in the cellar went bad."

The cab slowed.

"She's a good woman," said the cabbie. "A good wife. The best wife."

"It's always in the water," said Mel. "This sickness, the fever."

"I don't have a wife at all," said Mike.

"Shut up," said Mel, "I want some quiet to cool my head." The land was perfectly flat. It tilted hard up and ramped toward the mountains and up at the sky, except there's no such thing as sky, it's only a word. The cab rolled on between sand and sky. Slow, slow, careful. The cab blinked red, metal striking metal, right right right at the A-frame half a mile ahead.

"I'd like a house with red curtains," said Mike.

"Dengue fever and hemorrhagic fever," said Mel, "They're the very same thing when you get them."

Mike said, "I'm tired of this night."

"Bleed out your ass, then die," said Mel.

The road made an X in the desert with the gatehouse, and here was the gatehouse with gate and soldier. "We're not turning in," said Mel. "Tell him. We're not turning in just yet."

"Things aren't so foolish as you think," said the cabbie. The cab coasted and slowed to near stopping. The sky hovered as usual. "Lock his door," said Mel. Mike slapped down the knob, the cab rolled slow into the X.

The soldier stationed at the gate had seen the headlights coming for miles. Flat has new meaning in the desert. He'd thought Duluth was flat, Minnesota was flat, but no flat is flat until you've stood in the desert at night and seen headlights at fifteen miles. His mother had sewn his name in the back of his shorts. He had rubbed his backside and watched the headlights come.

He had tucked his clipboard under his arm. He had slipped his pen in his shorts to warm the ink. He'd snugged on his helmet. He'd stepped into the cold and stamped his feet. He'd go far in the service. His mother said his father had said that. He would ship in three weeks with two thousand souls and some other boy would stand graveyard at the gatehouse. Once, long ago, the soldier had sat by a tree. He'd watched a squirrel on a branch and also a large bird, which flew and hovered. It was after that squirrel. The bird had swooped and pecked and the squirrel had parried and slashed. There must have been something in the nest. The afternoon had passed that way: the soldier picked his teeth with a twig, the sun dropped down, and when the soldier's hand found a stone of handy size, he'd flung it, "Quit that squabble," and the squirrel ducked and the bird flew up and away. They were back at it before long. The soldier took a nap in the roots of the tree. His helmet hid his face.

It was four miles per hour at the X, but the needle dropped below 0 and sat there quiet.

"Tell him," said Mel. "Tell him before he turns." The cab stopped in the X. The soldier at the gatehouse saluted the cab and waved it in.

"Keep driving," said Mike. "We'll stick together." Mike held the pistol at the cabbie's neck, a silver pistol with a big black hole for a mouth.

"Like he said," said Mike, "We're driving out."

The cab revved through the X. Ran through north. The soldier at the gatehouse stepped back, tucked his clipboard and watched it go. The soldier at the gatehouse will make Major after two tours. He will marry a girl from Roswell who will lose her liver to a virus, a cure found the year after she died.

The cab rolled on the narrow rough road beyond Base. A car had not passed that way for thirty-six hours and fox and deer scattered in surprise from mile to mile. The mountains loomed. Mike held the pistol close to the cabbie's temple when the cab slowed or weaved to the shoulder. "Steady on, Ricardo. Steady on."

"I'll have a pack of kids someday," said Mike after a mile.

"Sure," said Mel. "You'll take them on field trips to visit those caves."

"I don't care for caves either," said Mike. The cab rolled north and north. "He's never going to like you," said Mike to the cabbie. "He just can't."

The soldier at the gatehouse watched the taillights a long while. The right blinked right for miles after he walked back to the A-frame, which was warm and bright. A mouse ran across the floorboards at 0400. He might bring the General's cat. The moon made a new cloud silver and the soldier took a paper and wrote a letter that mentioned the cloud. The tail-lights rose and fell ten miles out, crested again in twenty, he yawned at one hundred miles, right right right, a jet floated down, the landing gear was tinted green red green. In a hole, some tail covered its nose at the jet sound. A lizard licked the air with her tongue.

There was no turn at mile 109, but the tracks in the sand started there. The tracks cut east, fishtailed through succulents and creeping vines, wound around the cactus. The tracks were plain as day in the last of moonlight until the wind ate them.

"My dad's in the field by now. He's fighting with that plow."

"He'll get a dog."

"What good's a dog?"

"Dogs are fine."

Mike drank the last of the bottle and threw it out onto the sand.

"A nice home for some bug or mouse," Mike said.

"They'll cook in that bottle by noon," said Mel. "Some friend you are."

"Jungle men cook bugs and mice from the mud in a bottle," said Mike.

The cactus gave way to the tires and grill. The cab lunged and weaved through sand.

Once, Jim White kicked over his lamp by a pool. That was darkness! The useless lamp rolled to the edge and rocked there on the lip. Jim dropped to his knees, if there were such things as knees. He groped in his kit. The bats screeched in their usual way. Jim's fingers fumbled, the box burst open, and the matches fell to the ground.

Way back, this desert was an inland sea. Those mountains were coral reefs with caves big enough to fit a town. The reef hugged the eastern shore, eel and sharks, the sponges and urchin had children who grew up and had children who died on the reef and it rose up fine and tall with all their corpses. Fifty million years, lava spit and lava cooled, great lizards slept on islands. One day, the sea dried up. The land filled with sand in a blink. The reef was gone. Then two hundred million years. Jim rubbed his leg in the dark, the real dark, and a real leg with a real boot on the end of it. This desert was once an inland sea and Gloria tripped on the foot of the table. Just a little sprite. Of course there was blood, the girl had cried, any girl would have cried, but Jim had groped the ground and found her tooth. Time passed, ten million years. Jim dipped the tooth in the pail till clean, the roots of the tooth were exactly like a screw. He held her head between his knees, the small glorious head, one million years passed, and the reef busted out lean and sharp, those mountains there, brown and pretty, a girl's round belly, round as a melon on account of breakfast, and screwed that tooth back in her head. An inland sea: where the deer and mice ate the grass, grew fat and died, a tree grew from the guts, then the wind smoothed down the ridges and ribs and knocked over the tree. A mountain soaked in an acid bath hollows at the roots like Swiss cheese, it all makes sense. Jim was hungry by the cave pool in the dark. He ate a leg of roasted chicken from his kit. His stomach growled. It unsettled the bats.

The cab cut east some miles. The moon set. The searchlights lay down. The cab halted nose up on a dune that looked exactly like a cresting wave. Mel got out and kicked the tires. Mike sang a marching tune, the stars faded to a slice of sun.

"Get out and dance," Mel said. "You're a happy man."

"Something with local flavor," said Mike, and clapped a drumbeat. The cabbie stood by the dune.

"Like a wedding!" said Mel.

"He's stubborn," said Mike.

"Make him spin." Soon after, Mike spun the cabbie.

"Tie his hands." Soon thereafter, Mike tore his shirt, wrapped the head in his right sleeve and the wrists with the left.

"Now, give him a kiss goodbye. We best get walking."

"I'll not," said Mike, but he touched the soft temple above the sleeve. "Sayonara, amigo," he said.

"On your knees," said Mel. Mike pushed the cabbie down.

Way back, this desert lay at the bottom of the sea, ten million years, or some time, the reef rose and fell, the acid bath receded, and there in the end were caves. Rain and snow dripped and prettied them up: columns formed where drippings met; the gypsum chandeliers were unsurpassed. When Jim's fingers found a match by his toe and struck light, Jim kissed his own hand. The fishes in the pools thought it was the moon. The caves are grander than the pyramids on the Nile, more lavish than a cathedral in Rome. These caves are so big as to fit ten cities, with balconies and bridges of gold and pearl. The caves' ceilings, too, are something to look at. See there, fanged and curtained, towered and peacock-tailed, pocked, razored, fancied and filigreed over every silken wall. See here: every inch buzzing nectar, now cold as lava, from yonder buttress. There, the apple-pears bangle from a marble girl's arms. Behold and wonder: The stone bear licks great stone paws! There, the winged snails sleep in lace forever in mother's kitchen garden. Ten-foot turtles stampede, off to war, and with what speed, while their golden riders squint and aim for the spleen and pit of the tall sweet terrible sad. The world is full of beauty! The world is full of beauty! I am down on my knees to tell you!

They spent one bullet on the cabbie. They spent one match and the rest of the shirt on the cab. The fire was pale and disappointing at the beginning of day. They emptied their boots and retied the laces. Mel wiped his nose, which was blue and smeared and sore. They warmed their hands as the frost dripped off every thorn and made a damp place in the sand that a flea would drink up in a week. In one hundred years it would be a puddle of respectable size, in ten thousand years, a pool with a fish. In seven hundred thousand, a modest lake, ten million and fifty-two, a smallish sea and the caves drowned.

"I wish I had my belt," said Mike. The boys got walking south. They would have followed the sun but some clouds had come in. They turned their backs to the mountains and followed some animal's trail. They looked up for jets.

"They must have been grounded."

"Maybe they'll send dogs."

"We'd hear if they sent dogs."

The cactus pointed the way. It was far to walk and they tired. Some bats flew up from nowhere, as if the bats could stand it no longer. They turned east, maybe they were birds, they turned west. Far away a thing cried out. Sand beat on their faces. They turned north, then east again, behind a still ridge of rock. They walked south since the sun was high, the ridge rolled over and settled back down. They took turns with the sombrero. The red balls on the rim glowed in the sun, joyful and good.

Up north, a farmer planted his field seed by seed in black dirt. He saw no mountains at all. The tractor coughed and the farmer stopped on the third pass to lift the hood: the boy ought to have changed the oil. A black fly buzzed his ear as he tinkered. The farmer waved with his hat and slapped at his neck and when the tractor turned the fourth row, a rocket ship flew over. A black fly crawled to his nest, happy, with the lump of farmer's neck in his thorax.

"Good morning," said the man on the trail. The man was neat and trim, but tall as two men with hands big as plates. His trumpet was gold and tied by rope to his belt. His skin was red, but by nature or by sun, it was impossible to say.

"You better come with me," the big man said. "You boys look lost!"

"We have to get back. Can you help us home?"

"Of course, I'll lead you," said the big man. "But first, come see a wondrous sight!" He lifted the trumpet and played.

They turned with the big man toward the mountains. He told all about his life: his gal back home who was fine; his last best meal which was sausage and beans stirred in one pot. He told about his late great horse and many other stories. "Such successes form a man's soul," he said. The stories did lighten the mood.

The boys walked on and on. They tired and rested sometimes. In this way, the day passed. A gull flew over. They looked back from time to time and smoke curled up from their abandoned fire, as if they'd not walked a mile.

They suffered and shivered, but the big man did not break a sweat. Once, he offered a canteen and something that looked like bread. They did not sleep at night, but walked. Another day came and went, seeing double, like crabs, and a third day and a fourth. On the fifth day, the big man whistled in a pair of seahorses from the green pasture yonder: twelve feet at the shoulder, one dappled, one bay. They'd been nibbling clams. They were less than keen on the bridle, pawing the grass and tossing their heads. These were no gentle steeds. But the man was firm and they came to him. He called them deary and sweetheart, and my-precious-little-one. He petted their thick rough muzzles. He fed them sugar from his palm, which they licked clean with footlong tongues that curled and forked and roved his enormous forearm. In this way, the beasts were made tame for the journey.

Rabbit's Foot

"Fight on the roof!" A steel door slammed above.

Tommy clapped his hands. "Let's go." He jumped two steps at a time and Billy followed skipping three steps at a time up the stairwell to the roof party.

The fight was more of a skirmish: two guys, one girl, someone's dog. It was mostly played out by the time Tommy and Billy slammed through the door. The contestants were still chest-to-chest at the burn barrel. Snow was falling on their jackets and their hoods were pulled up.

"Hey, Tom," people said, and Tommy said, "Hey."

"Be good," their mother, Rose, had said a thousand times. She spoke loud in Polish to her seven boys and they all understood.

"Come on," said Tommy to his little brother.

The fire in the barrel burned old kitchen chairs. People were breaking them up with their boots and other people were stuffing the chair parts in the flame.

"We should build a snowman or something," someone said, but no one did.

There was snow on the TV. The extension cord was completely covered up until it appeared in the gap under the stairwell door and snaked away to some plug-in below. A La-Z-Boy collected snow on old leather. A girl with a blanket watched a sports channel, pitches in slow motion, a jockey tossed off his horse over and over, trampled over and over, commentary, golf scores. The stereo speakers thumped. The people stood in groups near the edge and swayed and drank and laughed in the green light of the hotel sign high across the street. Billy shifted his eyes just in time. Girls clustered, an amoeba, or a many-headed amoeba with smoke from its nostrils and slanty mouths. Or a dragon. The girls weren't pretty. He'd thought they'd be pretty. The pretty ones turned to check Tommy out. Billy was still just a kid. People and girls sat on the brick ledge swinging their legs over pedestrians four-floors down. Billy tied his laces. He zipped his coat to his chin. He breathed on his hands and made friends with the stairwell wall.

The card table was in the middle of the roof under a saggy beach umbrella. It was lit up by a construction work lamp that someone had dragged up there. Buckets were turned over for seats. Tommy was looking over the players' shoulders. Tommy wanted in on the game but it was the last hand before intermission. The hermit crabs had arrived. The crab handler had a brown bag he held over his head. He circled the table. When the hand was over, he dumped ten crabs on the table by the potato chip pile. Some crabs balled up in the cold. The live ones were going everywhere on the table between the bottles and half-empty cups. The derby would begin momentarily.

"First one to the edge wins," someone said.

Tommy put ten dollars down to buy into the derby. He picked up his crab, chugged his beer, and drew the starting line with cheese whiz. The crabs lined up. Tommy's was medium-sized, built for speed, black and healthy looking.

Tommy said, "My crab will kick ass."

He chugged a bottle that was near.

"He's Billy Super Crab for my baby brother."

A few people looked over at Billy on the wall. Billy liked peace. Billy was scrawny, fourteen and slim, but taller by the day, a rocket on the launch pad at T minus ten seconds.

"On your mark, get set . . ."

They were off in the first heat.

The flag over their building was only a block and a half away but MIA in this snow. Billy closed his eyes and could see it anyway. The flag was the same year and model as Neil Armstrong's moon flag. Same dye lot, same bolt of cotton. Their granddad's company made the moon flag. When he died, he left Rose a stack of backups. The boys would divvy them up when she died. They were folded in plastic in the front-room closet. Rose was conservative with replacements. She made repairs until there was no other option. But if too much city grime had caked the cloth, or if cracks had formed along the stripes, or if the field of blue began fading into the stars, Rose went to the closet. She shellacked the fresh flags on the fire escape for fumes. They dried on the grating in the sun until they stood straight out like zero gravity. When the flag was absent for repairs or replacements, the old neighbors yelled complaints.

"Billy, where the hell's our goddamn flag?"

"Sean, tell Rose to hurry it up with Neil Armstrong."

Rose had the boys rig up a spotlight system for night-time viewing.

Billy could not see the moon either. The snow. The smoke billowed thick from the burn barrel and people's liquored breath made him dizzy-headed. He would never see grandpa's original. Hardly anyone got to go to the moon.

People gathered under the umbrella for the second heat. Billy Super Crab had won the first heat by better than five lengths, though three other crabs never even stuck a leg out to try. The money on the card table was divided with little controversy.

"Give it to me, baby," said Tommy, and he kissed his crab for luck which stirred the crowd.

"On your mark."

Billy inched off the wall.

"Get set." He stepped closer.

"Go."

A boy might walk the ledge on his hands. A cartwheel. Billy inched closer to Tommy's back. Billy stuffed his hands in his pockets and watched the racers go. When the race was won, he opened a beer for himself.

Billy Super Crab kept winning.

"He's a natural athlete," said Tommy.

"Mine was half dead when it got here," said one of the losers. "I should get my money back."

"Whine, whine. You got to want it. My guy wants it more."

"Shut the fuck up."

"I could tell it about my boy first thing I saw him. He's serious," said Tommy.

"Shut the fuck up," said the loser.

"My little brother's my rabbit's foot." Tommy nuggied Billy into the circle under the umbrella. "Fuck off, all of you."

Rose's magic child was born at the beginning and end of the astrological calendar, her Sweet William. Future President of the USA, and bulletproof. Future baseball star, a left-batting righty, future badass of Wall Street. Future ball-buster, and rich. Horses and pull-tabs would obey him someday.

"Come on, baby, come on."

Super Crab triumphed again.

"How old are you?" said one of the girls.

"Seventeen," said Billy.

"You're taller than your brother."

"Two inches."

"Your brother's mouthy."

Tommy ate pretzels like a bear. He belched and the girls laughed.

Billy Super Crab won the sixth race and the seventh. Someone turned the music off. Most contestants were in permanent hibernation, eaten by the dog, or lost in the snow with the dog digging. People were shivering. The beer was colder and they drank it fast. Only three crabs were still going strong. One guy offered a twenty for the Super Crab, but Tommy said, "Hell no."

"More beer."

A half-pretty girl showed up and Tommy knew her. She leaned in like Queen of the Rooftop. She stood by Tommy.

In the next race, Billy Super Crab pulled away in the last six inches beating out a little orange speedster who came from nowhere.

"Super Crab, Super Crab, Super Crab." They pounded the roof with their boots and threw peanuts at the third place finisher who had not moved from the starting line. He gazed at the chips like warm sand, but Billy knew dead eyes. He drank. He picked up Mr. Third Place, blew heat on him, and put him in his pocket. The sirens whined across town in a swirl of blue flash far away.

Rose made only boy children. She said she didn't want girls since this world was a bad place for girls. Making boys was easy, she said, pound fast and hard for a minute and a half, and no more. It took five minutes at least to make a girl, and some pleasure. Billy's dad slept on the couch in the front room. God had been nasty to Rose, she said, but it skips generations and a boy was a good thing to be: like the ending of a Sunday matinée, she said. Like the pilgrims in Technicolor starving for months and months then fine and saved when the Indians finally show up in loincloths. The big beautiful brown men enter from the edge of the big screen. Feathers and fancy leather. They have arms the size of Rose's front door. The arms are looped around huge baskets of bread, and dried fish, and late red apples the size of this boy's head. It is the camera angle. The enormous feast is set at the pilgrims' table, grateful, THE END.

In the second feature, Martians pack for travel at low velocity. Back home is far, Rose said. The mission is not really over yet either, since part of the mission is just looking around, hovering. Meanwhile, over at the saloon, the black hat draws but the white hat is faster. The ladies swoon while townsfolk watch the last loop of the last reel.

Billy pulls off his shirt under the marquee. He stretches in the summer sun and yawns. He reconnoiters with his brothers at the corner and they cut down alleys, over fences, between buildings, then they pick up speed through the old bat's yard just because they have all day. Since the old bat's got her own patch of grass. Since the old bat doesn't have to share. She stands in the window and hollers, "I'll be calling Rose about this private property infraction!"

"You do that, lady!" Alan calls over his shoulder. "See what Rose says! Hope it's in Polish!"

They stomp instead of walking. They clang chain-links and kick cans instead of stomping. Pretty soon Teddy's making up a song which doesn't make sense but it's funny as hell with every cuss word known harmonized with the seven: Paddy, Matty, Alan, each louder, Teddy, Sean, Tommy, and Billy the loudest since Billy is the loudest word in the English language.

"More beer."

Billy Super Crab was ready for the final. It will be sudden death against the only other crab still on its legs, a big pink-shelled bruiser twice Billy's size. They were calling the challenger Pussy Crab for his losing record. Some guy was pissing on the ledge. The Queen of the Roof whispered something in Tommy's ear. He tipped his head and slid his crab-cold hand up her shirt. She had no coat on.

"Super Crab, Super Crab, Super Crab."

The racers were off fast. Pussy and Billy neck-and-neck. Billy was finally getting tired, he hesitated on his legs. His crab eyes shifted right to Pussy who saw his chance and surged. Then Billy collected himself. The crowd leaned in for the photo finish. Both crabs went over the edge but Tommy was on the spot. He scooped Billy from midair, held the champ overhead, and pumped his arms.

"The winner!"

"Super Crab, Super Crab, Super Crab!"

Pussy bounced off. The dog barked.

Of course the race was under dispute. The construction lamp crashed over first. Then the table and everything on it. Tommy was after a big guy who was mad about everything and Super Crab went flying. The dog was running around and didn't know who to bark at. Arms, fists, the usual, but the fight was green in the hotel sign that was extra dim from several missing letters and old bulbs too, while the crab was lost under all of this mess with only his ocean shell for protection. It had nothing to do with him. Hopefully he would tuck and hide, wait it out, what shells are for.

Billy the Boy crawled on the ground. He reached and swam and groped amongst bottles and bills, chips and heels, cards, cords, glass and thighs and parts he wasn't supposed to touch yet.

He called out, "Super Crab, Super Crab, come here, boy."

Billy planned to be a huge man someday, six-foot-ten and three hundred pounds of pure, good, unadulterated Bill. He would walk through town and it would move aside. Their dad was small and mean, a little mean dog on a long chain, and they moved aside. He never worked a full day; though his office had papers in piles, no business was transacted there. He kept a diary in the front room, locked, which Paddy Jr. would inherit along with the key around Dad's neck. The seven stayed clear of the front room on the first of the month, when rent was due, and when the bottle was empty by the couch. They took the back hall to the fire escape. He sang in the shower. Nobody starts out mean. Everyone is born clean and good, a little pink baby with a smile in a carriage and fresh skin and pink lungs to cry out with. Once a cow died in the creek on Dad's father's farm. Before the men came for the carcass the brothers played a game with the cow. Oldest to youngest they ran and jumped and bounced off the spongy cow into the water. Dad was last. By his turn the cow was deflated. He fell in the cow and was pulled out by his brothers. He smiled whenever he told this story.

"Go fuck yourself," Tommy said to the guys who had him now.

Billy crawled toward Tommy's voice and found him in the dark.

"Better have his parachute ready," said a bad voice with bad laughter. Two guys had Tommy hogtied at the arms and legs. A third man had Tommy's belt buckle, laughing and barking. The guys staggered with Tommy under all his thrashing. Billy pulled on the leg-man nearest the ledge.

"He won't even die," said the hand-man.

"He'll die," said the leg-man, and pushed Billy off him. "Get him off me."

"No, I heard of a guy who fell from six thousand feet and lived," said a hand-man.

"You're high," said the leg-man.

"Guinness Book. Look it up, shithead. Landed in a cornfield," said the hand-man, then the swinging got synchronized. "Broke every bone, but lived."

"There must have been a tree or something he fell on," said the belt-man, who was holding off Billy with a free hand.

"Watch it, kid," said the Queen. She was on the hand-man peeling his fingers.

"Hey, get this kid, get him off me."

"There was no fucking tree, look it up," said the hand-man. He shoved the Queen. "Hey, get this girl off me. She's impeding our work."

Now the Queen was on the edge tugging Billy, who was tugging the leg-man who swatted Billy like a fly.

"Billy!" called Tommy.

"Look, he's smiling."

"Get this kid off me. That's not smiling."

Someone lifted Billy, kicking and biting, from behind.

"Tommy!" called Billy.

"Man-who-fell-to-earth, it was a special on TV," said the hand-man. "Jerry somebody, a postal worker. Broke every bone."

"Freaked the cows," said the belt-man, who must have weighed a thousand pounds, ten thousand pounds.

People were laughing, watching the show, and rolling around.

"I bet that postman guy goes to church now."

"Someone get this kid. I mean it."

"Paddy! Sean! Teddy!" called Billy. They would be pulling their coats on as they ran for the door.

"Shit."

"Hey, easy, easy," said the Queen on the arm of the leg-man, who pushed her off. She fell on the La-Z-Boy.

"My back hurts," said hand-man. "I'm done here."

"We're not done," said the leg-man. "Not even."

"Alan! Matty!" called Billy, their boots stomping three flights down to the Lincoln sidewalk with the flag and a net for circus jumpers.

"Swing him higher," the leg-man said, "I hate this little smiling shit."

"Hey don't, hey don't, hey don't!" said the voice of the Queen, dusty and sooty. Then Billy fell.

A satellite circling within earth's gravity is falling the whole time.

He fell for an hour, equals forty boys back-to-back, or twelve girls with some pleasure.

The air was nice. The snow slapped his chin.

A fly is the lowest thing always repenting.

A siren for a meteor a mile wide crossing into Polish gibberish.

"Billy!"

"Rose!"

The rocket blasted past the blue ambulance stairwells.

Mother would cry, don't cry. Dad will be dead in two years, I promise.

The snow will be one hundred feet deep, I promise, silky like flour.

Brothers with nets, yes.

Flowers, yes.

Dragon girls, yes.

The headline: Miracle Boy.

No cornfield or cow.

Super Bill, Sweet William.

Out of my way.

No Name Creek

On the way to the truck Ben prayed his prayer in case it might help: please, God, whoever you are, last day of moose season and the freezer's empty.

"Ready, little brother!" said Boak and revved her.

"Ready," said Ben.

Ben slammed the passenger door. Fine. Fine. Shit-kickers on the dash. The water boiled in the thermos for later. The yard needed raking but would wait.

Boak floored her.

Ben: groggy and sluggish. Map in pocket. The rifle in the jump seat. A bluebird day for raking.

A slap hard to the meat of the thigh.

"Wake up, little brother!"

"Just drive on," said Ben. He rubbed his leg.

The sun came up over the bar, then firehouse, then the truck turned. At the T, Ben goodbyed Boak and Sue's, a little blue house still sleeping with the mailbox open and the front door closed. Once it had just been Sue. Sue at the T this, Sue at the T that, the new gal in town, and no Boak whatsoever. When Ben still had a chance.

"What?" said Boak.

"Nothing," said Ben.

"You were always a mumbler." Boak bit at cake from some bake sale.

"I said nothing at all," said Ben.

The truck missiled out of town.

Boak chewed, crumbs fell, and Ben wiped them to the floor.

"Some bull is ready to end his days!"

Boak yelled it with the cold windows down.

A hunt is a tiresome thing. A moose is big and unaccommodating: fifteen-hundred pounds, tall as a shed roof, well-hidden as needed. He likes to browse and chew and sleep and gnaw and live.

They drove the morning with no success, drove, bumped, groused, walked, drove on farther, turned, bumped again, groused again, slogged, aimed, reloaded, and cursed their luck. They saw cows galore in the willow browse, and their calves too, so easy for the taking by the despicable. At Crooked Creek it was grouse, more grouse, and a mateless swan. At Puritan nothing, a porcupine. Dry Creek, rabbits, got one with the truck, didn't notice. Ermine Creek, birds and birds, seagulls, but why? The sea is far away from here. Why bother asking, who cared? A fox, but Boak missed and laughed. At Heartbreak Creek, nothing, a yearling bull with velvet horns, and they let him go by the book. Washout Creek, nothing. Goodbye, nothing. Winston Churchill, nothing.

"Damn it to hell," howled Boak when granddaddy bull popped in the alder on Doubleback. But the shot was high and that's why they call it hunting.

They drove north and gassed up at noon. Ben found a penny in the men's room. Boak found the man with the bull in the flatbed and made friends at the pump.

"Nice one," said Boak.

"Lung shot," said the man.

"Help us out?" said Boak. "Last day."

The man swiped his map from the dash and tapped with his finger on what looked like nothing. He made an X with a pen and circled it.

"Can't miss there," the man said. "It's a regular zoo."

"What's it called?" Boak said.

"I never heard. She's too little for naming," the man said.

"All right," Boak said.

"You boys try it," the man said, and he and the bull turned south.

Ben watched Boak and the man with the bull on the flat-bed from the Coke machine. There was the big glass window. The Coke machine was empty. Ben waited hand on hips, nose to glass.

Boak: good-natured face, balding with ball cap, goatee, shit-kickers, Wranglers, knife on the hip.

Please, God, whoever you are.

Then Ben and Boak were driving again, looking for moose.

In the north the sky was clear. A bluebird day for driving. The road was empty: trees and trees and a yellow dashed line. A few trucks passed and saluted with hands. The boys saluted back and Ben counted vehicles, each of them going by, for miles.

"One," said Ben.

They swallowed cold coffee from the station. Styrofoam squeaked beneath Ben's boots. Sinatra sang on the tape deck. The truck rumbled warm and sleepy and the yellow leaves fluttered and smoothed the pavement, which was a conveyer running to its end. Ben sang along with Frank until Boak pinched them both off with his fingers on the dial.

"Can't Miss Creek," Boak said. "Zoo Creek."

Trees and trees. "Two," Ben said as a semi passed.

"Granddaddy Creek," Boak said. "I like the sound of that."
A hill passed.

"Nice Guy Creek," Boak chimed. "Gas Up Creek."
A dozer passed aimed west.

"Three," Ben said, getting sleepy.
The sky. A dull sky.

"No Name Creek," said Boak. "That's what, that's what."
The road twisted and straightened. Trees and more trees, a house, a barn. A gas station boarded up, a culvert crushed by something even bigger. A fire engine sped south without the siren and waved.

"Four," said Ben.

"Last Day Creek. Where's My Moose Creek. I Got Mine Creek," said Boak and laughed. "Ha ha ha."

Once at Mother's, Ben drank milk from a glass and it was delicious and cold. But before the last swallow, he felt a thing on his tongue: a shave of glass long as a nail. Ben showed the glass to mother. She shook her head and made batter for morning. Ben kept the glass on his sill by the jar with the lucky pennies.

"Five," said Ben at a Harley whizzing up and by.

Once, Boak kicked a baby pool out of his way.

"How Bout Lunch Creek," said Boak.

Ben grabbed the sack of deviled ham and Swiss from the back. They drove north and chewed like twins: twin mouths, twin noses, with exact matching rotation. The hands rose from the elbow with the same angle and thrust.

Hills and trees, lakes and birds, hills and lakes. A bird alone. A flock. A flock and an eagle on a phone line sagging. Can the caller on the phone hear eagle's claws? Hills and hills. A bag of trash in the ditch.

"I Gotta Piss Creek," said Boak.

They pissed twin arcs at some pleasant-looking birch. They drove on. The road bent toward the mountains parting swarms of black spruce up the slope.

"Makes me think of winter," Ben said to the high white.

"Of course. It's October, little brother. What kind of dope needs whitish mountains to tell him that?"

The peaks jabbed at the sky and the sky just sat there and took it.

The station man's creek ran up the rusted rail line to the Pass. Parallel the rails, the truck growled in low up the road that was really no road at all: just two lines of dirt in the brush that kept going. The cliffs climbed and made the day end early. The truck bumped and dragged and stalled and revved and wallowed in mud pits between. A moose ran by while they fussed with the winch. They passed many signs of life, all long dead: a locomotive off the tracks and in the trees, a cedar tank dripping rain at the rivets; a station house with a coffee can roof and a sign that said MINE YOUR OWN BUSINESS.

"Mine Your Own Business Creek," said Boak. "Mine your own business. Mine. Your. Own. Business."

They passed a handcar on a side rail toting green bottles. They passed a pallet with black punky cordwood, leather boots unmatched and tongueless hanging from a clothesline across the back deck of a caboose, trees chewed down, a beaver lodge built, lump coal in a pile, logs stacked and tarped, a ball of rebar big as an outhouse and twisted like some kid's joke. More coal. More rabbits. More trees. More Boak. He rolled down his window and spit.

"We aren't idiots!" he yelled to the Pass.

The rifle jumped off the jump seat any number of times. Ben righted it again and again until he wedged it between the seat and the bag of deviled ham and swiss. The road curved up and up and on along the railroad tracks. Another station house came and went in poor condition: its canned roof was caved and the walls were unreadable. The creek wagged and zagged by the boys like a friend. The eagles circled and swooped as was right for them to do. The eagles sat in tree-tops and snags when their wings got tired and watched the tiny truck driving. The headlights off. The sun was so west that the boulder, when it came, spread in the road as big as any blue whale. The boulder had tumbled from that cliff, five-hundred feet down. The crack in the mountain was just so wide, very narrow in fact, with no room for boulders rolling on and on and on. The boulder had flattened the rails like a penny. The boulder would sit for a million years. The rails would rust. The boulder had jumped from the cliff and flattened the rails on a day no one saw and no one remembered. The rest was just guessing.

"I guess it's a bluebird day for walking," said Boak.

"I guess it is," said Ben.

The truck shuddered dead at the boulder. The boys shouldered their gear and got walking.

A Pass is a big cut that doesn't end where it looks to. It just goes over the other side. They walked by a shot-up Ford with a fridge door leaning on the headlight. By a tree with one leaf left. By a bush turned red. By a bush with berries. By berries in shit.

Ben thought this:

Mountain: tall, rude or greedy on occasion, made of stone thrust up from elsewhere, terrible, sad, OK, invincible. Useful for poems.

Cliff: rock like a fence.

Rabbit: a small edible mammal, plentiful, friendly reputation, big families.

Magpie: a clever bird, black and blue, steals dinner if able and doesn't care.

They walked and walked. Once, Ben was called to jury duty and heard this story: A man was gone three years and his wife wanted the insurance money paid. He was last seen on the ferry from Skagway in a mask, tank, and fins. Now what about that? Now what about that?

They kept walking and whistled.

"That scuba man was not for sure dead, I'm sure."

"What?" said Boak.

"Nothing," said Ben.

Trees: tall, usually unselfish, of variety and kindliness, carbon, sometimes terrible, sweet sad, appearing invincible to some but vulnerable to axes, old age, lack of sustenance, fire. Useful in cold.

"What were you saying?" said Boak.

"Nothing, that scuba-man trial."

"Oh, yeah," said Boak.

Heat rises and cold sinks. The cold sank.

Hand: a necessary appendage.

They passed by a butte and by a gorge with a waterfall with no name either. They heard hooves pounding, branches snapping. Ben ducked, Boak fired, but the game was safe, gone in the darkening trees.

They passed by a rusting wheelbarrow, pouring nothing out sideways, looking like a crab.

Bear: top of the chain so will eat you or part. Good for stories at gatherings and postcards.

"Goddamn It Creek," said Boak in blue gunsmoke. They walked.

Boak: puckered when sweating, long strides like no tomorrow, gloves always deep in butt pockets, shaft on shoulder, straight like a Roman, half step forward like a queen gets to lead.

Poem: a set of words put together to say something that can't be said. Ben once slid one in Sue's mailbox in his best pretty longhand, but Ben's longhand and Boak's longhand were perfect twins.

Mix-up: a mess that causes the wrong or undesired result, brought about by fear or happiness or love or an absent mind or poor penmanship.

Sue: pretty, sweet, nice, sets her chin on her knuckles while listening. Gap-toothed. Holds her head while laughing hard.

Mix-up: a terrible mess brought about by poems. Boak won that one too. Boak always won.

"Wins what?" said Boak.

"Nothing," said Ben.

"How the world is declining," Boak said. They shook their heads at injustice. The brothers walked on, sweated and walked. They heard gunfire the next drainage over and walked faster.

Leg: a necessary appendage, needing another.

When the boys were young they played charades with friends. First, they did presidents and movie stars, like everyone, and the notable people in town. But as years passed and the boys grew, they took on greater challenges: a barn door, the kitchen sink, the curtain in the bedroom. The boys progressed to trees by species and cloud formations and diseases of the body and mind. Boak stopped there, but Ben aspired higher: to local geologic formations. He would stretch his arms, stand or squat, tuck his head or throw it

back, fling a leg, turn the wrist depending on necessity and
art. He peaked like Granite Peak and Castle Mountain. He
lounged into Lazy Mountain, thundering into Pioneer Peak,
a spitting image of Gunsight. He crescendoed into Denali,
greatest challenge in a few continents.

They passed by a helicopter between some trees. One ro-
tor was ripped off.

"Some crash," said Ben. "I'd love to get her home."

"Get her flying again," said Boak.

They considered with hands on hips.

Then Boak aimed, fired, and made a fresh wound in the
sheet-metal tail. He handed the rifle to Ben who blew away
the remains of the windows. They squatted and drank their
tea by a huge old ribcage. They wiped their mouths on their
sleeves. The sun sank. In the ties, they found the femur to
match to the ribcage.

"Gigantic."

It had snapped in half long before, between steel wheel
and steel rail.

Then the hip, "Enormous."

Then the jaw, "Stupendous."

Then hooves, "Only three," all dragged, gnawed, and left
hither and thither by some hungry someones. Gunfire rang
out farther off. An owl called and another answered.

Head: a fragile clumsy sphere, teetering in space.

It's hard not to think and Ben thought: Once, on a
summer hunt as boys, Boak and Ben came to a camp on a
shore where the men laughed and the bitch barked and the
puppies were cooked up in a drum. The fire was rotten and
the stirring was done with a broken paddle. A man found
it on the rocks. The boys were offered the pick of the litter,
ha, ha, ha. The boy Boak had cried. Death is a cricket by a

creek. A million dead, a million born. A million dead again. So on, and yet. The willow is eaten, the moose is eaten. The fish never swam home. A blue whale yawns. A foot crushes a nest. A tremendous hoof. A splendid club. A bird hits the windshield, chaos of nature. A man drops from cancer, age, or accident, is forgotten, and never was.

Ben dug in the gear for the headlamps. He flicked one then the next on off on off on.

"Quit," said Boak, and Ben flicked them off.

They walked.

Neck: a necessary and narrow conjunction between body and head.

Ben: a good-natured face, balding with ball cap, shit-kickers except on Sunday, Wranglers, knife on the hip, strides like a thing with a tail.

"It's getting dark," said Ben.

"My brother the genius," said Boak.

"I mean it," said Ben.

"Keep walking, little lady," said Boak.

"It's a long way back," said Ben.

"We've got light yet," said Boak.

"We should turn round and go," said Ben.

"But we won't," said Boak.

The shack had the porch light on. The generator was buzzing. A dog was barking, people were moving around. A stupid little dog. The boys ducked behind a handcar parked in the splay of the tracks as the porch door opened and a man in an apron appeared for a smoke. The man puffed and the boys watched and the stupid little dog barked louder. The man threw the stub and slammed the door. They backed out of the clearing and kept going.

"Stupid dog," said Boak.

"What?" said Ben.

"Nothing," said Boak. "Just a stupid dog."

With the shack far behind and real dark near, Boak started up his singing:

"Riffraff. White Trash. Stupid Dog. Copter Bog. I'm a Hog! Creek!"

"Quiet," said Ben.

"Where's My Moose. Give Me The Noose. Hey, A Caboose Creek!"

"Quiet, I said," snapped Ben. "I'm tired."

"Tired Boy! Tired Boy!"

"Pipe down."

"Pipe Down. Why the Frown!"

Ben stopped walking altogether. He slumped on a stump.

"Someone should Pay. Anyway. Make my day CREEK!"

He watched Boak over the rise and listened to him disappear: "Look this Luck, Stuck in Muck, Should have got a Duck Creek!"

Bliss among humans is rare. In the morning of the best day and the worst, a man does not know it. And how to tell them apart?

Once from some shrubs back home, Ben followed paw prints he had never seen before, even in books. These new paw prints were pressed into new snow. They made tracks from the shrubs to the pond and crossed. They were a barefoot baby's feet, curved in, with pretty fragile lines, but giant: the size was a man-sized foot. The giant baby had walked down to town. It had turned corners and crossed crosswalks where boots then trod over its going. The baby, Ben could see, must have turned around from time to time to look back at where it had come from. Must have stood pigeon-toed at the drugstore window, then continued on to the bandstand in the square where Boak and Sue had wed, then to the fire hydrant by the courthouse curb.

Ben liked to go barefoot.

When Ben caught up on the flat, Boak was winded and spent. The rifle was ready, serious again about the task.

The wind kicked sand and they turned their faces into it.

Boak said, "Who makes them up then?"

"Makes what?" said Ben.

"Who decides the names?" said Boak. "Who get the say in what the name of the creek is?"

"Some guy in an office in town," said Ben.

Boak started up more whispery: "Dead Dog. Red Dog. Red Neck. What the Heck. Clap Trap."

"Who cares anyway?" said Ben to the sky.

"Crap Shack. Shitty Dog," said Boak.

"He writes the name down on a paper," said Ben.

"I Can Smell Him Creek," said Boak.

"He stamps the paper just like that," said Ben and stamped his hand with his fist.

"I Can Taste Him Creek," said Boak.

"Some fool stamp," said Ben.

"Come out, brother," said Boak.

"Puts the paper in a drawer," said Ben.

"Show yourself, friend," said Boak.

"It's in the drawer forever," said Ben.

"Show yourself!" said Boak. "Show yourself!"

"People go somewhere else entirely," said Ben.

The stars blinked awake. The sun was gone behind a pink edge for good. It happens every day.

The bull stood huge between the railroad ties. He turned his rack on cue. Boak fired for the lungs. The bull went down in a heap.

"He's had a setback," said Boak.

They stood, then ran. They stood over him and gaped. They gaped at the long way down the Pass, which was almost too dark except for light in the shack far below.

"Must be eight miles," said Boak. "I'm tired."

"Maybe seven," said Ben.

They sat against the bull. He was hot and died. They leaned on him and drank their last tea. They chewed cake from the bake sale and smiled like girls.

"Long night," said Boak.

"A good day," said Ben.

The beams from the headlamps prodded the black. The fur and his face. The old bull stared out too. Night lowered and the last of the pink faded.

They slit him open, pulled his insides out, and quartered him quick. With the rack he was eight hundred pounds easy. They threw the guts to the trees. They piled his parts off the rails just in case. They wiped the ground with their fingers, then lay between the rails for a nap. The wind picked up. The stars were the Big Bang all over.

On Ben's best day, there was a moving van in it, a little blue house, and the T: a big heavy box with Sue's thin arms around it, saying "FRAGILE," on the side, so true. A blue print dress. Sue teetered past the mailbox. Ben jammed it into neutral, dead center of the T, Ben blocking traffic just like that, King of the Road. Ben ran up the walk to Sue. Ben making the save just when Sue's arms were about to give. The mailbox, the doorstep, the threshold. "Oh, thank

you. Oh thank you oh so much. It's my mother's china."
Sue could not tell the difference between them then. Boak
or Ben, Ben or Boak?

The trucks backed up at the T in all three directions. Sue
held her head while laughing hard at the trucks.

"Your truck's still running," said Sue, and Ben looked
and so it was.

Once Ben saw Sue's face in the paper made with a thousand tiny dots, first prize for jam. Who can find anything
when it's really lost? *Yours sincerely, Ben. Sincerely yours, Ben.
Always and Forever yours, Ben.* It's Ben. I'm Ben. And so
happy, Sue, to be Ben.

"A guy should ride him down," said Ben in the dark.
"That's how."

"That shack," said Boak. "Those handcars."

They stood and looked down on the bull's face. They
threw the gear by the moose rack.

"Hate to leave him," said Ben.

"He's not going far," said Boak.

"Seems tranquil," said Ben.

"Others will want to sample him," said Boak. They looked
around and at the trees for watchers.

"Best be quick," said Ben.

"Let's go."

The boys ran the first mile at full steam. Their lights ricocheted off tree and stone, down and down and down.

The windows of the shack glowed but the generator was
off. The racket inside was louder, music blaring. The door was
propped with a five-gallon bucket and the dog's nose stuck
out of it. They slipped among the handcars and picked the

one they wanted. They hid when the man came out, stood, and whistled a tune.

They pushed the handcar up the tracks the long way. The ground froze with each step. The moon rose high. They leaned and strained and pressed and sweated and groaned and wheezed. The cliffs gleamed. The headlamps flashed on the rails. A man gets tired. They grunted like pigs made of bone and gristle, skin, tendon and teeth, up and up, and no one there to see them suffer.

"A long way," said Ben pushing. Ben felt bush in his gut: red and hot with thorns. He knew it was there, but he didn't. The tendrils reached and rubbed Ben's insides.

"So far."

The bush burned his insides: his arms and ribs, rooted in his thighs, it fingered his lungs and squeezed. The crown of it shoved up and choked him alive, hot and cold.

"It's hurting," said Ben, sweating and puffing.

"What, Ben?" said Boak, sweating and puffing. "It's a long way up."

"Sure," said Ben. "Heavy forever."

Their headlamps reflected in the moose's eyes. They wrestled him in over the rim of the handcar: like the scuba man sitting on the bench by the handrail. No whale in sight for the scuba man. The world is big. Gravity is fast and fair. Like falling back in gray water, ready to breathe through his mouth, falling to the judge in black, the bench splitting and spraying spit over the deck and duffel, alive, gray water inviting, Come in and live here, scuba man! Come in, come in, whoever it is you are!

"That was a good idea," said Ben, flinging a thigh. "Two can be, one can be, or two can be one. That scuba man had all he needed."

"What?" said Boak. He was heaving the moose ribs, so heavy, Ben had to help.

"Nothing," said Ben. "Her freezer's full now."

They loaded the gun and gear. Ben found a spruce limb for a brake. He tucked it under his arm. The trees were white in the moon.

"A great ride."

"Yes."

They leaned on steel and ran. They left the snout by the tracks as if to watch for trains.

The True End to All Sad Times

Evening rush hour and Marlon squinted at the 32 out-bound. It was late. The bus lollygagged one block south at the corner of 6th and Franklin. Marlon waited in rubber boots at Washington. The slush was thick. The evening was cold with horns, cars sliding, nearly colliding, fishtailing, spit and sputter. Second shift came on in forty-five minutes. He might still punch in on time.

When the Franklin light turned green, the 32 roared through the intersection.

By nature a bus is a vehicle with an amiable face. It belched blue and the haze flew up bluer between soaring glass, steel, brick. The city was sticky and hard. For example, if a guy didn't notice the white ground or the winter-bare trees in the median islands or the manhole covers rusted and steaming over the city's seal, or pedestrians' purple mouths steaming and chattering at the stop for the 41 or 56 across town, or the taxis' smoking tailpipes, or people smoking in doorways, arms crossed against the bitter cold, everything cold, or if a guy weren't able to fly up over the city, for example, to re-connoiter the world from above, to examine the icy tangled streets, how they grabbed and held together, how they webbed out, out into frozen gray highways in the country, gaffing the towns and cities and tethering them together into one great raft, he might think he were alone on a hot day in the Sahara.

The 32 blinked as it sped the block. It changed lanes.

The girl would get on at Lincoln. The girl, the girl.

Marlon did not like people. He squinted at a star between black towers. Marlon loved this star. He loved the cracked glass in the doors of the 32 as it rumbled to a stop. He loved the decisiveness of the snow, how clean and neat. He loved George Washington best of all the Presidents for his Cherry Tree, though the man would never have been Father of Our Country had he not been so tall. Just another cotton farmer with bad teeth. Marlon loved the Bluebird in sneakers painted on the side of 32 and its sisters in the metro fleet. How they flocked busily and helpfully about town. How wonderful.

The 32 shifted right, nosed straight at Marlon, and accelerated.

He loved his skin and body in theory. But once a red mole popped up on his neck, and when a man at work said, "Marlon, you have jelly on your neck," and pointed at the mole, Marlon hurried to a stall in the men's room and, facing the toilet, twisted it off. Marlon squinted when trying to understand things. People at work thought he just needed glasses. His bushy eyebrows prevented him from appearing ungulate on first glance. He had one hair in his left brow that never stopped growing. Marlon loved this hair more than any other part of him, though he knew it was wrong to. At present it was five inches long and resisted tucking into the brow. He used Vaseline to keep it down or an equivalent. He kept the mole in an envelope in his desk. It turned black. He tried to love it anyway.

The 32 lunged when it stopped, and splashed. Snow was predicted with temperatures dropping and high winds revving up over night.

The bus doors snapped open. In the big round mirror, the fat driver sat amphibious on his throne chewing pink gum.

He fiddled with his foul left ear with his foul left hand where a foul gray audio wire came out of it, sly like. Jowly. Over-flowing. Marlon had dissected such as him in biology back in high school. The driver bobbed to invisible bass and drums. His lips, teeth, and tongue snapped and licked. This driver looked down at Marlon standing in the slush. He blinked and subtracted Marlon instantly. Deletion is painful.

Marlon fingered the pocketknife in his trousers.

He stepped from the slush up the steps of the 32. His coins clanged into the steel box.

The driver's name tag said "Boone," but Marlon knew this name was a lie. A name is just a word and can be concocted for show or effect. "Boone." Once, "Boone" hit and killed a calico cat at the corner of 6th and Hoover. Marlon was the only rider in the 32 at the time, the only witness. Hate is like a rock in the dirt that a guy finds when he digs deep enough with a shovel.

The 32 took off and Marlon swayed down the center aisle.

Dear Mr. Bluebird Metro:
I am a regular customer on your bus line service. I take the 32 out to work at 5:10 Monday through Friday and back downtown on the 2:33 AM, the last bus. It is hard to complain. I am not a complainer by nature but

"Boone" parked his car on BB, the lowest level of the metro lot, space #429, and was often the last metro employee to leave at 3 AM. An earthquake or terrorist attack would crush the small car easily. Rat poison, enough to kill every living thing on earth, could be contained in one average sized water tower. Marlon dreamed of retaliatory deletion: in the elevator down to BB and a lead pipe; in the bushes in front of the driver's rundown apartment building by the river with a pair of scissors from a Hitchcock movie about love and jealousy; in his favorite coffee shop, a Styrofoam lid, a syringe; between the yellow lines at #429, a maul from the thrift store for a dollar, wiped for prints and dumped in the donation bin later that night after the deed was done. The yellow would slant parallel, but the yellow paint on the concrete was not permanent. Grease and blood on concrete were not permanent. Nothing was permanent. The girl at Lincoln was permanent.

His mother was permanent. Way back, Marlon's mother had given him the pocketknife for Christmas embossed with the word M A R L O N in gold script over red enamel. At work, silverware and cutlery were commonly stolen from the break room. Marlon's knife had often saved the day in break room emergencies: blocks of cheese needed to be cut, for example, a salami log, celery and carrots for the dieters, a cake on someone's birthday. His thumb had since rubbed away all the letters but the M A. Once Marlon had a dream of subtracting himself of his arms and legs. He lived on a cart with wheels and a pull cord for a puller. A bad vision to wake up to, but he attributed it entirely to the driver. Marlon did not believe in dreams.

The 32 rolled along.

Marlon sat, as always, in the seventh row back on the left and watched the "Boone." The man next to Marlon at the window wore all black clothes: new slacks, jacket, scarf, overcoat, and an old-fashioned felt hat too small for his head that must have belonged to some other older man. He wore sunglasses with lemon yellow rims even with the sun almost down. He tipped his chin in the air as blind people do and Marlon knew the man must be blind. He held a thick pile of legal-looking papers on his lap. His fingers rested on the mute lines of type. Marlon craned his neck and read Whereas,

Whereas, Whereas written in bold at the beginning of each paragraph. The heading at the top said Last Will and Testament of someone. The paragraphs were totally surrounded by white space, by nothing at all. Marlon felt sorry for the man and the white spaces. The blind rode free on any Bluebird Metro. They got on first, got off first, even before the pregnant ladies and the old folks with walkers.

It stopped at Adams, a President who, history has proven, loved his wife more than the Presidency or power. An old man climbed on, gave the driver a dollar bill, then kept walking up the aisle to a seat by the emergency exit in the way back. The driver stuffed the bill in his pocket, a crime Marlon had witnessed from this "Boone" more than once.

"Put it back," Marlon said. "It's a crime."

The driver grinned greasily and waved in a pretty girl in a peach parka who did not pay her fare. He gave guff to a kid in a hockey jersey over some nickels, then the nickels spilled and the hockey kid was on his hands and knees grasping for nickels under the driver's chair, between the gas and brake, nickels splayed over dirty rubber as seconds passed, a half minute, a minute or more until the hockey kid began to cough as the exhaust boiled in at the door, which was still open, blue haze seeping up the stairs as if to smother the hockey kid.

The blind man covered his nose with his scarf.

"What's the holdup?" said the blind man who seemed to look for the source of the trouble. His face was calm.

"Suffocation," said Marlon.

"Loose change," said the intercom.

Marlon coughed, "My God, my God," and pressed his nose to a crack at the base of the window where the air was cold at least, but still tasted of tar and smoke until the hockey kid dropped the nickels in the steel box, and the door snapped shut, and the 32 pulled forward, only to wait again for some children jaywalking with their dirty clothes, something, who knows what is hidden inside any cinched laundry bag?

Then the bus rolled on.

The blind man's phone rang in his pocket but he closed his eyes behind his glasses and didn't answer. Marlon took the opportunity to squint at the blind man's paper: a silver set including all trays and servers to be passed on to, twelve Wedgwood settings to be divvied up between, a wedding dress to be re-pressed, re-vacuum-packed, and shipped to, a sterling football charm bracelet to be soldered and polished to be donated to, an international thimble set inventoried and delivered to, a Wagon Wheel pattern quilt in blue and white cotton, stitched in 1824 by a long dead Dolley to be cleaned, repaired, and passed on to the loving daughter, etc.

Marlon quit reading when the driver refused a lady with a stroller, telling her, "Too wide. Collapse it or wait for the next bus."

The lady was yelling. The lady got off. This was why the world was failing.

The driver did not remove the foul gray audio wire from his ear during the altercation. The driver bobbed his head, which sat atop his thick neck. The skin: folded, white and soft, double-soft, double-fat, doubled up below the fat ears and fat chin. Gum-chewing bobbing "Boone" "Boone" "Boone."

The shaggy shelf at the back of the skull. It slopes so suddenly to the neck. How easily a blade could enter that slot. Oh, the skull is nothing either! A thin shell over a bag of pudding! Any decent pocketknife has three distinct blades: one long and sharp for entry in the fleshy parts, one jagged for sawing, one small and neat for trimming fat. A hand could choose any, you see? The job is the thing, the purpose, the location of entry to be determined by simple Homo sapiens rife with flaws. President Taft, for example, was the fattest in the White House. Once, his men dislodged him with butter from his tub. White House staff installed a bigger one, 500 gallons. He walked with a cane made of petrified wood, 250,000 years old, imagine, imagine, Marlon told the blind man.

"That's old," said the blind man.

"Yes," said Marlon.

"Don't let that driver get to you," said the blind man. "He bothers everyone."

Blind people were wise. The 32 changed lanes past a stranded taxi, driving too fast, of course. As the cross streets flew by, Marlon stuffed his knife back in his pocket. He wrote up the incident in his notebook citing date, time, and location. Waiting for the other riders, he was able to finish the last few lines of his latest letter:

> *Dear Mr. Bluebird Metro:*
>
> *First too, let me explain that I admire Bluebird. I know you are busy. But enough is enough as they say. You are the man in charge and I'm a man who cares. I am a credible person. What is truth? What is decent? What is true is everyone needs all their senses attuned and running tip-top for driving the public in a metro bus. Eyes and ears. Focus, civic awareness, obviously. The law is on the public's side. Please note: "No driver of any city vehicle shall employ any device or implement that impairs or could impair in any way his auditory abilities or function while operating any municipal vehicle." IS 646.82.7(D)(a). Further, no driver can elect to let riders ride free except those authorized by law, like the blind. Or to deny legal riders, e.g., young mothers with strollers. But these violations are occurring. It is happening on Bluebirds every day, sir. Egregious I can assure*

you with proof and records. Please rectify. It is bad for the
morale of the city.
   Thank you for your consideration.

The new riders settled into their seats and the 32 sped away. It stopped soon at Jefferson, the red-haired drafter of the Declaration of Independence.

She would get on at Lincoln. She had red hair too but going gray. She had been riding the 32 for seven years. She averaged every fourth night so she was overdue. In school, she swam the crawl in lane four during practice. She sat two seats away in biology sophomore year. Once, when the student between them was sick, she and Marlon had silently dissected a baby rat together that was not dead yet. She had handed him the sharp implement for the liver and he had brushed her finger in the handoff, which was small, pink, and agitating like the rat. He had backstroked and butterflied in lane three or five all those years, as near as possible. In history class, Marlon got all A's and one semester sat right behind her and smelled her hair day and night. Thomas Jefferson owned a slave girl name Sally who gave birth to untold numbers of red-haired babies. Despite his numerous A's, Marlon learned this shameful fact only after high school. He was angry at his teacher for the omission. This teacher had also said Marlon could be president of the USA if he wanted it enough. But Marlon wanted many things.

The 32 departed Jefferson with teenage mothers with toddlers crying loudly.

The 32 stopped at Madison. A gang of new riders came on and none of them paid a dime. They milled around near the NO STANDING sign and talked to the driver. They laughed as if they were all friends. It seemed unlikely. Marlon wondered. The old man and the hockey kid played

Guess-Who-I-Am in the back. They got loud sometimes with an occasional guess yelled out: Al Capone! Sinatra! Gretzky! Bugs Bunny! Peels and snorts of laughter until the intercom boomed, "Pipe down!" All strangers, Marlon considered, playing games and piping down at the "Boone" command via the "Boone" voice through "Boone" pipes running the ceiling of the 32. From indecent lips to the decent ears.

"Anyone can get a job driving a bus," said Marlon.

"Anyone with eyes," said the blind man. "And a driver's license."

"It's hard to swallow," said Marlon and the blind man nodded out the window at the world. "The power in his two hands."

"The stupidity," said the blind man.

"The injustice," said Marlon.

They nodded. Sympathy felt wonderful.

The blind man's phone rang again. He ignored it.

Anyone can get a job driving a bus: it had been just a theory. To test it, Marlon had once taken a day off work and gone to the third floor of city hall where a woman with bags under her eyes and a seeming-constant-headache handed him the paper. Her small desk was ringed with smiling family pictures. The paper said: APPLICATION FOR METRO-BLUEBIRD DRIVER. Felons drive public buses for years before they are discovered. Child molesters have a difficult time finding steady work, for example. The lady on the third floor also received all the completed applications, glanced at them, dropped them into cubbies marked YES, NO, or NEED MORE INFO. After that, Marlon thought much about betrayal and the Rights of Man.

When Marlon got down and out about life, he thought about the girl. He closed his eyes and pictured her standing in the glassed-in stop in front of the tall, bronzed Lincoln who pointed at the ground with a longer-than-natural finger, drawing his line for Emancipation, etc. Her red hair under her tight wool cap. Marlon would spot her from a block away. She would have a magazine rolled up in her pocket. The driver would unplug his foul left ear, in deference, as she ran up the steps. Her wild animal eyes would knock Marlon over hunting for a seat on the 32. She might sit in absolutely any row at all, any seat, so unpredictable was she, his angel.

When they married, Marlon would get the ring from his mother. It would be silver with a row of tiny diamonds leading to a ruby of some size in the middle. Old-fashioned. The tarnish would rub off with skin and matrimony. They would honeymoon in Fiji. They would eat from wooden bowls with knives and forks inlaid with mother-of-pearl. They would snorkel with Australians and hold hands underwater as fish of every color swam by.

They would live together in a small town with a water tower near the courthouse. There would be a pool at the high school and they would swim together in the mornings. The belly of the water tower would be hoisted in the sky like the belly of a pregnant queen. The place would be named Chillicothe or Greely or Eureka and the word would be painted across the belly in a script expressing the personality of the town. Marlon would keep his job at 7th and Van Buren. He would take a different Bluebird and would rid himself of this driver entirely, forever. She would keep her job until the kids were born. There was a town called Marlon, Idaho, in an atlas and they would go there on vacations in a minivan. She would take his picture in front of the city sign as a joke. She and he would swim next to each other in lanes three and four at the pool while the kids took their lesson. Everyone would bob and cluster at the side of the pool, talking together. The old ladies from town would wear bloomer suits and swim in lane one. They would admire the kids and offer to babysit as their pendulous breasts floated weightlessly in the lovely blue. But it wasn't blue water. The blue was just the color of the paint on the bottom of the pool. The water might have been purple if purple was the popular color for water, and trendy. The pool would contain all the town's fluid and feeling: sweat, spit, semen, blood.

The 32 stopped at Monroe. No one got on or off. Marlon petted his eyebrow down. The blind man seemed to study the paragraphs on paper, but that was impossible.

The blind man's phone rang again and this time he sighed and answered. He smoothed the papers down with his free hand.

"Hey, Desmond—Thanks, yeah, I'm real tired, that's how. You don't want to know—I just went over it with the lawyer—Millie got the quilt—Betsy got the silver set—Yeah, sure it's worth more. Betsy won't care. She wanted the quilt, Dolley Madison's. Tighten your seatbelt—all this shit—Desmond, you have to tell her for me and—You've got to. I can't right now—Better you than me—OK, I owe you one."

The blind man clicked off the phone. "Fighting like cats," he said to Marlon.

"Sounds like it," said Marlon, shy and nervous at this sudden friendship with a blind man.

"Sixteen years of this," said the blind man. "Who cares about a quilt?"

"Dolley Madison was a Quaker," said Marlon. "She became a widow via yellow fever. It killed her first husband and her infant on the very same day."

"My sister and my wife, they hate each other," said the blind man.

"What can you do?" said Marlon.

"Not one damn thing," said the blind man, wringing the papers.

"You should tell those two about Dolley Madison," said Marlon.

"I might," said the blind man.

"About real suffering," said Marlon. "About how time is short."

"I will," said the blind man. "I'll tell them."

"Good," said Marlon.

The 32 stopped at Quincy. People moved in and out, briefcases and backpacks. A lady with a bag of green apples sat just across the aisle.

"Everything works out, I guess," said the blind man and Marlon said, "Sure," and thought how this was a very noble position for a blind man to take.

Polk, Taylor, Fillmore.

Streetlights under stars. The half-moon popped between buildings and disappeared. A blaze burst up from a grease fire at a street vendor's cart and the man's face glowed for an instant. People walked, ran, milled, clustered, and broke apart in black bundled shadows. A bundle of newspapers burst open in the wind and the pages cartwheeled in feathery sheets in the headlights. The city whizzed by. Windows and doorways blinked and the sky darkened. From the back, the hockey kid yelled, "Yankees." The old man muffled his mouth laughing. "Sox," then "Ahab," then "Osama Bin Laden."

"My mother grew up around here," said the blind man. "She's dead."

"Oh, I'm sorry," said Marlon.

"Your mother dead?" said the blind man.

"No, she's not dead," said Marlon, which was not altogether true. "I hope the weather holds."

"Yeah," said the blind man seeming to actually stare out the window, which Marlon knew was entirely impossible.

After graduation, Marlon heard through alumni contacts that the girl had married Rich at Six, the meteorologist from Channel 7. Several years later, Marlon's contacts confirmed the marriage had gone south. The couple was separated and was possibly divorcing. Rich had been "Richie" in high school, then just another regular guy on the swimming team. But Richie won the state diving championship in 1972—a long shot for victory from the high dive. He nailed a maneuver never seen before or since, called "the Bomhold" for Richie's last name. Witnesses still disagree on elements of the dive and in which order they were properly performed. Marlon was on the bench and remembered it this way: Richie had climbed the ladder, pale and grinning at the crowd with a poor kid's crooked teeth. Pulling himself up the top steps, he sprang onto the platform. He strode to the end seeing his future. He turned and wiggled his feet backward out to ready position over nothing. The judges gripped their pencils. People in the bleachers sat up from their tropical slouches, suddenly and unexpectedly expecting something big from this no one. Richie sprung backward out up into the empty, flew up to a spectacular height, pinnacled dangerously near the gym roof, then snapped himself in half, twisted, spun projectile, twisted again, unsnapped himself, tucked into a ball, flew like a planet forming its own orbit and no sun at all to bother about, then he thundered down, and just as he parted the water, he appeared to burst into pure hot flames. No splash at all. Richie disappeared under flat blue water.

Rich came out at the ladder tan with capped teeth, slicked-back hair, a two-button blazer, the weatherman's wand in his dripping hand. Of course she had married him.

"Actually, my mother's dead," said Marlon.

"Oh, I'm sorry."

"I don't like it," said Marlon, "that she died."

"We're in the same boat," said the blind man.

"She gave me this," said Marlon, presenting the pocket-knife from his trousers.

"Real nice," said the blind man, who seemed to look at the knife, also impossible.

"I'm glad the blind get discounts," said Marlon.

"I agree," said the blind man.

The 32 honked at a car turned sideways. The car gave the bus the middle finger.

The shadows ran across the cross streets.

They passed Rich at Six, pixilated and nine stories tall, glowing across an old brick building. Rich's hair was slicked back, just out of the pool. His weather wand was twenty feet long: "DIVE IN WITH RICH AT SIX," was the electronic banner that turned the corner of the building in never-ending loops.

"I wish I had a wand," the blind man said.

"Me too," said Marlon.

"I knew him in high school," said Marlon.

"Very interesting," said the blind man.

"He was popular even then," said Marlon.

"I believe it," said the blind man. "My wife Betsy loves that guy."

Rich had a bus-sized mustache, a locomotive jaw with train-track teeth and a baby-pool-sized dimple.

"Why do women love him?" Marlon said.

"Hell if I know," said the blind man. "But if they bottled him, I'd buy a case." They dreamed up brand names for Rich's new drink: Rich at Six's Cyclone Tonic, Hurricane Cola, and The Bomhold Elixir.

"I like you," said Marlon. "You give me a good feeling."

"Ditto, buddy," said the blind man.

They shook hands and then their hands parted.

The blind man's phone rang.

"Did you tell her?—And?—Oh, Jesus—She break anything?—God damn it—I'm on the bus—Put her on—Well, tell her to pull herself together and call me back."

The blind man hung up. The blind man took off his lemon yellow sunglasses and rubbed his eyes, which looked like anyone's eyes. They stared at Marlon's eyebrow, but that was impossible. Marlon smoothed his brow. He glared at "Boone" in the big round mirror, still bobbing and chewing as if nothing mattered.

> Dear Mr. Bluebird Metro:
> Say something. Say something.

The blind man's phone rang again.

"Betsy, sweetheart—I'm—I know, Dolley Madi—But think about it, sweetheart—Don't talk about scissors at a time like—You wouldn't do that—You're talking crazy—I know you wouldn't. My mother's favorite—No, Betsy. No, Betsy! I totally forbid it!"

The line went dead. The blind man stared at the phone and put it away. The 32 rolled on. People squirmed in their seats.

Marlon squinted. "'In this sad world of ours, sorrow comes to all,'" he said. "Abraham Lincoln said that."

"Very apt," said the blind man.

The lady across the aisle eavesdropped and chewed a spotted apple, smiling.

"What are you smiling at?" Marlon said, turning in his seat toward the lady. She bit the core so that seeds were revealed in white flesh. The driver grinned in the big round mirror where the passengers all grinned tiny grins wrapped in scarves and hats and hockey jerseys. Why do they all smile? What's the joke? What's so funny?

"I'm sorry for all your troubles," said Marlon.

"Thanks," said the blind man, then reached and touched Marlon's sleeve.

Guess-Who-I-Am ended in a huff when the hockey kid picked a rock star the old man could never have known. The blind man blew his nose. The stars jangled in space. The snow was holding off. So far, the weathermen were wrong.

The girl got on at Lincoln.

Her red hair was pulled up in a bun. She read her magazine in the fifth row right. She had been the prettiest girl in school by a long shot. She was forty-five years old now.

At Johnson the 32 sat in a traffic jam at the convention center where a horse show was starting next week. Cop cars swarmed the intersection amidst a mess of crushed steel and scattered glass. A horse trailer was on its side. A man on a stretcher waved his arms. A black horse with an arched neck skittered on the corner. An officer held its bridle. Two bays burst from an alley. People chased ropes. Hooves skidded in the sloppy street.

The girl called out, "Oh no, oh no!" at the horses.

"There's a dead one," said the intercom.

A passenger was crying in the back.

"The poor things," said the blind man. "I hate to see suffering animals."

The police came on horseback. Gates arrived in sections, one by one from the convention center off-ramp, one man on each end, around the cars and buses, through the crowd, then pinned together at the hinges for a crooked corral.

"Look at this crowd," Marlon said. "Hungry for misery."

Eventually, an officer waved the 32 through.

She got off at Harrison, not her usual stop, a tone-deaf President with a cross-eyed First Lady.

She ran on the sidewalk. Marlon watched her run off.

Years back, he'd lost the pocketknife. It was this same sloppy time of year and Marlon punched in late with freezing fingers. The flaw was simple: a hole secretly formed in Marlon's pocket. His coworkers said he'd never find it. On break, Marlon had taken a flashlight for the search. He had backtracked. He had crossed and searched opposing corners. He had picked around the pits made by cellar steps, searching and never losing hope. There were no spectators when he found it. He had stopped to tie a boot under an awning. There it was. No cheers or backslaps when he held the knife in the air triumphant. Perhaps a better life was coming. Perhaps finding only required bending and reaching. Perhaps her love will be full and full of compassion as it was for injured horses, for stray dogs, he guessed, waiting in alleys beside trash cans, hoping. Perhaps he will buy her flowers once a week. Perhaps roses or daisies. Perhaps the florist will say, "But sir, we have no daisies," and Marlon will answer, "Dahlias? Thank you. Keep the change."

The 32 sped away from her.

Perhaps the water towers will be filled with delicious Elixir with spigots at the bottoms and words across the enormous bellies, in both English and Braille, instructing: "Drink here: For the True End of All Sad Times."

"Goodbye," Marlon said to her shadow running. "See you soon."

Hayes, Garfield, Arthur, Cleveland.

Nearing McKinley, the blind man stood. He squeezed out of the row past Marlon.

"Good night," said the blind man. "This is my stop coming up."

"Good night," said Marlon.

The blind man swayed down the aisle. As he turned under the big round mirror, Marlon was seized with sudden joy and gratitude. He could not contain himself from calling out: "I'm sorry you're blind! Blindness is the worst of all disabilities!"

The blind man had begun descending the steps. His hat and face were still just visible. The blind man stopped and turned.

"You've overcome blindness beautifully," Marlon added. He covered his eyes with his hands to demonstrate, then uncovered his eyes, like the blooming of a flower.

The blind man stared.

"Blind!" said the intercom.

The lady with the apple giggled. The apple was just core now.

Other passengers whispered.

Marlon stood in his row. "Blind," he said.

"No," said the blind man, and shook his head as if this was very sad news.

Marlon moved into the aisle. In the big round mirror Marlon appeared to be shrinking smaller and smaller, until tiny, then tinier, a diminishing dot, melting to minuscule, dissolving to microscopic, absolutely into nothing, completely, whatsoever.

"Not blind?" Marlon said.

"I can see everything," said the blind man.

When the bus bumped, Marlon swayed in the aisle, swinging like a man in a tree.

"Sit down, you idiot!" said the intercom.

"Leave him alone," said the blind man on the steps.

"No backtalk to the driver!" said the intercom. "Even if you're *blind*."

"I've had enough of all this picking and tearing," said the blind man. "Of people being nasty to each other."

"No yelling on the bus," said the intercom.

"Now look," said the blind man. "You just missed my stop."

The 32 flew along between Van Buren and Coolidge.

"You get off when I say so," said the intercom.

Marlon moved forward, up the aisle, toward the front of the 32. His hand pulled him forward as if swimming up through the seat backs. He grew with each step in the big round mirror. Several passengers stood for a better view.

"All riders must sit," said the intercom.

"Slow down!" someone called in the emergency row.

"This is my bus," said the intercom and snapped it's gum as Marlon arrived and stood under the big round mirror. No reflection was possible. He looked down the steps at the blind man. His papers had fallen, were scattered. He was on his knees over the papers.

"I believe in things," Marlon said. "I believe in things."

"Forget it," said the blind man, then to the driver: "Stop the bus. Open the door!"

"That's my door," said the intercom.

The pocketknife surprised everyone, even the blind man who had already seen it, who knew all about it and its history.

"Don't be an idiot," said the blind man.

Some screamed. The 32 sped on. The intercom laughed. Marlon's blade was small and dull. It cut the air like a conductor's baton, rising, falling. The 32 accelerated then fishtailed across Hoover, but did not shake the pocketknife free, or Marlon, who spun, as if a tree tossed by a storm. Some passengers stared in case they were interviewed later, noting his hair, the trouser descending into rubber boots, but missing the glint on his eyebrow. Some pointed camera phones—such footage was valuable—especially as a baseball bat appeared from a hidden space to the left of the driver's seat.

"Dumb ass," said the intercom and cracked the bat on the steel money box.

"Enough!" said the blind man who now steadied himself between the railings on the top step. "We need peace and kindness to live together successfully."

The bat jabbed. The knife danced back. They seemed at last to be enjoying life. No one would have predicted such dexterity in either. The driver jabbed with one hand, the other on the steering wheel. Marlon crouched like a bear. The knife flew out like a one-clawed paw.

"Shitwad," said the intercom. "The girl thinks you're a piece of shit."

Marlon lunged and fell back, lunged again undeterred.

When the first blood was produced, the 32 lurched and some passengers remembered their worst disasters: falls off swing-sets as toddlers, and running too fast down a newly paved hill until their face smashed on unpainted concrete. Some passengers remembered fears—public and private— draft cards, for examples, and worse, huts aflame in foreign villages. Failures: baby's bubbles at the bottom of pools, chlorine stink and sucking drains, and, oh how horrible, their most poisonous humiliations as the knife dove and the bat parried as if a demonstration of hopes and disappointments, attempts and rebuffs to kiss the girl, but she turned her head. Sad times never ending!

The passengers crouched. Some smelled final attics full of old dresses, or reached again between forgotten floorboards—the desired item as always too far, the fingers too short and only single-jointed. Some reconsidered stolen bikes, and pets in nooses, and mothers-in-the-arms-of-across-the-street fathers, and revenge, and moving vans, and caskets balanced on uncles' shoulders, and empty cupboards, and cupboards full of nothing good. Some passengers thought nothing. They watched with frozen faces. Marlon would have recognized all of them.

"You can't subtract me," Marlon said. "Only I can subtract me."

"Asswipe," said the intercom, but the face was no longer laughing. The face, Marlon saw, was just a fat man: gray cheeks and lips and piggy eyes. Sick and likely to die young of hardening arteries. Or electrocuted by wire in a tub. Perhaps no one cared about the driver either. Perhaps no one cared about anyone. What joy! What new release!

"I am multiplying," Marlon said to the ceiling of 32, to the now imaginable sky beyond it, between imaginably gorgeous apartments and heavenly clouds, "I am exponential." He stabbed the knife skyward.

"Mother-fucking pussy," the intercom said. "Mother-fucking psycho."

"Stop!" said the blind man, stepping between Marlon and the driver.

"I am as infinite as anyone," Marlon said. "You too will die alone."

"We will all die alone together," said the intercom. "Get over it."

The next moves were quick and blurry. The three men mixed together with a steering wheel, many-legged, too many causes and conflations for simple newsroom explanations, while the bat and knife intersected sleeves and skin and steering wheel. The 32 tossed with commensurate swerve and energy released. Passengers peeled at the window seams. No time for 911. "Let me out!" they called as the bus tires tipped and skidded, then jumped and straddled the median. A foot hit the gas. The apple core flew. The head-on occurred at Roosevelt, who, during his term, blinded one eye while boxing a friend.

The bus accident was the headline story at ten. The witnesses were sought to verify sequence, to opine intent, heat of passion by degrees, motive, history, too many questions. The horse accident ran second after the commercial break. A casino fire ran third since no one died, only smoke inhalation and fabric damage. Rich at Six rounded out the show. He did not yet know his personal connection to the leading tragedy.

Rich at Six made his reputation for extreme weather accuracy one Christmas Day. He predicted funnel clouds would descend on the region by noon, an unheard-of thing for that time of year. Some scoffed at his wand on the pale green chart. The counties all looked so apparently cloudless. He tapped the places of imminent touchdowns and waved toward depressions looming in the west. He foretold tornadic conditions, wind-makers too severe to quantify. The people were stunned as pressures built and systems weakened. "Go to the basement," he'd said. And they did it, though they knew nothing about him. Even CEOs took to the steps in their luxury buildings. "Go back! You forgot your TV," he'd said. They had carried down portables. They had plugged in under laundry tables.

Rich had said, "Watch this footage. This footage is amazing."

The people had done this too, though the footage was grainy: they'd watched a delivery truck blown over on the interstate. They'd watched loaves of bread in plastic bags tumble in the ditch, pushed here and there by wind.

Rich said, "Now, folks, imagine the morning."

And when the show was over, they turned off their sets and closed their eyes. They saw how birds would circle the wreck at daylight. Land by loaves. Peck bags for crumbs so close to asphalt, they'd have to lift their wings with each passing car.

For Swimmers

1. Drowning is unnecessary.

Ruth tucked a white curl under her cherry bathing cap. She wiggled into ready position on Slippery Rock. It was a perfect day for a swim, a bluebird day, a Lake Day as her father would have said. The water was calm and calling. It was May and the water was still very cold and he would have noted that too in his finger-wagging tone. Her father had been such a worrier. Ice just went out when? She did not remember. She was trying to forget things. There was nothing to worry about. Yes, she was very old, but she had made the round trip to Victory Rock a thousand times at least. This day would be 1001. Anyway, hardly anything was verifiable and certifiable, nothing entirely and completely. So true. She just wanted to swim. She had lived 29,997 days so far. So she dove.

Jim and his wife bought the place just north across Ruth's property line on Pike's Point in 1961. They came in May that year with all the other summer people and showed up every weekend. They were a friendly family. Just as soon as they got settled they invited Ruth down for dinner at their picnic table by the Lake for introductions, fire, wine, and congenial conversation.

Ruth was very welcoming to the new family, an attractive woman. She was so very independent. She knew she was just their type of person. She could see the wife admired her and so did Jim, that they agreed completely at first. She came from a big family in the area, Ruth told them. She toured them through the old family cottage on the Point. She, of course, knew everything there was to know about the Lake. Right off, she offered to show Jim, who liked to fish, all the good fishing places and Jim's wife, who liked to bake, the places where the berries grew biggest. Ruth was perfectly harmless to them and vice versa. In short, they all three looked forward to many years as friendly neighbors.

Ruth told of the rocks off their shore: Slippery Rock, Station, Three Sisters, Flat Rock. If you were a good swimmer you could navigate from one to the other out to Victory Rock, the biggest, and farthest—a monster of a rock out in the deep deep. Too deep and far for your little kids, she said. There was a man-sized V scratched into the granite where your feet went. The kids had called it Victory during World War II for morale and the home team.

Jim's wife did not like swimming, she told Ruth, and someone had to watch the kids. The next day Jim and Ruth stood out on Victory together, both up to their ribs in the drink and waving.

"Why's it here?" he said.

"Why's anything? It will be here until the next Ice Age," she said.

"Ice Ages are rare," he said.

They dove back toward shore.

The three new friends were always together. They sipped coffee and made cakes and meatballs. Ruth brought dusty albums of pictures: the cottage from 1908, her father and family by a fire and a horse, Ruth in Indian buckskin and braids, the Lake's record trout on the end of the line, and Ruth grinning in her canoe. On their whitest wall, Jim and his wife projected slide shows of places they'd been to: California, Yellowstone, and New Orleans. They unrolled maps of places they might someday visit. "Together," Jim suggested, with Ruth, and the women agreed. They boiled lobster and ate it with butter dripping. Ruth's face was a mess, "like a child," she laughed, and Jim dabbed her chin and lips with his napkin while his wife tucked in the children. They swam to Victory Rock daily and from Ruth Jim learned the contours of the shoreline and the underwater terrain.

At night they played guess-who-I-am and charades until late. They watched the waves during three-day-blows, violent storms that rattled the windows. It would rain and rain. The night trail between the cottages was a tunnel of wet and the flashlight tumbled its light up into the trees and made the strangest shapes. Jim and Ruth soon discovered they shared a strong weakness for each other. She laundered the sheets on Friday morning readying for the weekend arrivals and his midnight slide into her bed.

2. Don't swim far from shore unaccompanied by a boat.
Ruth paddled in the cherry bathing cap and no boat. The boat had been sold, when? Then she forgot the question. Most questions needed forgetting. She stopped to adjust the cherry cap. Red had been Jim's favorite and she considered blue. Station Rock was for a swimmer's rest. So the old lady rested.

Ruth's father was the first person to own land on the Point. He blasted the road in with dynamite when everyone else said it could not been done. He was a careful man and had a great respect for the water. "Anyone could drown in that Lake," her father had said, pointing out the blue window. "Best swimmer in the world." Then he told the story of his motorboat being swamped at Perch Place way back, and so on.

Father was a believer in rules and procedures and so for his children he had written out a list of instructions for swimmers. His warnings looped on the page like too much fish line in deep water. Six instructions in all. He had affixed the paper on the wall in the cottage under his photograph so unknown progeny would recognize the author. The corners were pinned. Four pins in all.

"My wife is not a bad woman, just not the right woman." Jim had said this more than once.

"Leave her then," said Ruth crawling on top of him. They had a wonderful time together.

"Give me time."

"How much time?"

"I don't know. Give me time."

"This is a once-in-a-lifetime thing," Ruth said and was absolutely sure this was true.

"Of course," he said and crawled on top of her this time.

Then the wife stepped in. Ruth lost many friends, of course, but had her family. Jim busied himself with work and family. He joined the planning board back home and took on many new responsibilities that gobbled up his time. His wife asked him to fundraise for the Save the Loon Society and he did though he cared little for the bird.

They both repented, but not completely. They swam by themselves to Victory. She watched him with binoculars from her screen porch when it was his turn. His midnight visits were rare and surreptitious to the extreme, but more romantic and passionate because of that.

3. It is sound advice never to swim alone even in shallow water.

Ruth swam and smiled at the quaintness of the rule and turned like a mermaid. Three Sisters. As kids they played tag in this triangle, diving between the one stone sister and another, one kid treading in the middle—The It. Inhale and hold it through the dive till you get there. Beware the clutch of the foot from below. She sat on the smallest sister and pulled her legs up. Triangulation and strangulation. To children, all that screaming and howling at the grab was fanciful, entirely outlandish, a farce. Maybe the wife was dead. People die every day. Such black fish come up from somewhere. So cold. She shivered. The dog barked, maybe it was Elsa's dog off its run again. Sound carried so far on calm water. SO FAR! Miles and miles or at the beach, that dog. One could count on dogs and rocks and beaches. The mermaid dove on to Flat Rock.

Years passed. Ruth made new friends, Elsa at the end of the Lake and a pen pal in Rome. Ruth met Jim in cities mostly when he was on business. On trains. They made love and fucked alternately, rolling and chatting in between about irony and telepathy. This while the sleeping car swayed and the whistle sounded. So strong, it was just a matter of time.

They had once argued about falling out of love.

"It can't be," she said. "If it's real love, then it can't be undone." This is how she thought then.

"Even if I never leave her," he said.

"You will leave her," she said.

Then Jim told her this story told to him by the friend of a friend: "A man and a woman were in love. I mean wild about each other. Nothing could part them. One day they drove down the road on an errand to a town they had never been to before. They disagreed about the best way to get there. She said turn left and he said right. To keep the peace he turned left, but he was still angry about it when, shortly after the turn, a dog ran into the road in front of their car. The man swerved and hit the dog. She left the man soon after."

"Everyone has a dead dog," Jim said.

"That's a horrible story and a lie," Ruth said.

"Just think about it," Jim said.

Years passed.

Jim came to the Lake less and less.

Once, for their anniversary, Jim sent Ruth a box of twelve chocolates and she was grateful. He sent a lacy nightgown once and she wore it at night in front of a mirror and turned this way and that way to admire the lines and potentialities. Once, he gave her a ring with a blue stone and she wore it on the left, even around town, until the letter. After the letter she wore it only to measure whether she was shrinking or expanding.

4. Don't stay in swimming until you are very cold.

She broke the surface at Flat Rock, which was three-quarters to Victory, give or take. Flat Rock was put in the Lake by some god as a couch for the miserable. She lounged. She thought of the nightgown and the mirror. Her teeth chattered.

Once, long ago now, the waves had come up in a passing squall and swamped her canoe not far from Victory. She had fallen in, a rarity. She'd lost the line and bait right away and her book on her lap had sunk fast, gone, an argument on fallout shelters and first strikes from submarines. Her hip-waders had filled. Down she went. Good practice for drowning.

On the way below, she saw a huge new rock she didn't know, had never seen, but how was that? A newborn giant just off her shore? This is not how the big rocks came to live here. No, it couldn't be, but there the huge new rock was!

"*Where is the mother? Where is its father?*"

"*They died.*"

"*Gone.*"

"*Gone.*"

The big bass had darted under the huge new rock. Wasn't that proof of the rock? A big bass swimming away, under the shoulder of the boulder? A big bass frowning hugely? One does not imagine a frown.

"*Concentrate, I tell you. There is only so much air in your lungs.*"

She had spun and turned away from the bass. She had fumbled with the wader buckles. Then came the threesome of land-locked salmon, a rarity. They had floated by after the bass, a fish parade. They had paused and watched her kick and tug for her freedom, but the buckles were just that stubborn.

"*Why not just breath in through your gills?*" *the threesome's suggestion.*

Bubbles and frowns.

"*Leave me be!*"

"*Concentrate.*"

She had squirmed one leg free from the waders, a lithe woman still. She had kicked airwards with the free leg, had risen some, then sank back down again. The leg was too heavy. The threesome of salmon had come very near to better study her troubles. They had turned. Then they dove toward a huge new gorge below. She had never seen this gorge either and stopped to study it. It was a thick, rough, new gorge cut deep into old gray lakebed. The gorge ran off into the murk, wide enough to eat her up, her cabin, every rock on the shore for a mile. So huge and still. Then she kicked harder, but still she floated down to it.

"*The buckle, the buckle. Attend to it.*"

In the end she outwitted the buckle. With both legs free, she kicked off the edge of the new gorge. The hip-waders dropped away. She floated up.

"Yes, I'm certain of the gorge. See?"

"I believe you. Swim hard now."

She pulled toward the surface.

"Good practice for holding one's breath. A full minute is above average."

"It's nothing. I've done at least twice that."

"Oh, you."

"Swim harder now. Kick and pull. Up, now, to air."

She kicked.

"But there have never been salmon in the Lake."

"I've seen salmon in my day. Swim."

She pulled at the surface. She did not look back to see if the hip-waders stood above the mouth of the new gorge.

"Swim harder. Your life is short."

"Yes."

The hip-waders sank away into the deepest deep. Never to be seen again.

"Who will you tell?"

"I'm telling you, old friend."

Or, if the threesome of salmon had tipped and followed the hip-waders down in.

"You won't die this time."

"Good."

She had dragged her canoe to shore. She had breathed more air than she needed and dried off with an old shirt from the knot of the tree.

She never found the new rock again, or the gorge, though she searched for both for years in her canoe, cutting the surface with her paddle and hands, digging holes in the Lake, and though she swam out searching with snorkel and mask, trolling in her stiffening body. In the end, she had mapped every foot off Victory Rock, two hundred feet in every direction, though surely the canoe had swamped no more than twenty feet away. She had circled, circling, had circled back. Sometimes she had rested on that old friend. Tracing the V with her toe, then diving off its ledge again. Once she had found the back cover of a book eaten at the edges on the beach by Elsa's. Had the canoe swamped on some other Lake altogether?

"Possibly. Such mistakes occur."

"A mistake?"

"A mistake."

Years later, she had reported the missing rock and the missing gorge to Lake authorities at the town office. She told the men her story and they nodded and leaned over subsurface maps. They said they would look into the missing geological artifacts.

"They might."

"It is wonderful they might look into it."

"I'm sorry for that rock and that gorge."

"Terrible, yes, to be missing."

On Flat Rock, she lounged a bit longer. The stone was a pleasant shape that hugged the hips. She snugged the cherry cap. Her legs dangled for minnows. The silly swimmers. Flat Rock was the most contented rock, with it's nose always just out of the water in this early season.

"But I am contented too."

"Of course."

"I have lived well," *spit and nostril.*

"Surely."

"Dying is just getting very cold."

"Yes."

"One must swim on."

"Indeed. Of course."

She pushed off Flat Rock. She kicked the shore away with her old feet. The Lake deepened. She kicked and pulled the last bit toward Victory Rock.

After reading the letter, Ruth went to the closet in the main room of the cottage and started looking for something. She found the following: poles and rods jumbled, reels, creels, baskets, bobbers, spinners and sinkers, tangled line; an old motorboat key tethered to a life preserver; her father's tackle boxes, uncle's, cousin's, all spilled out, decks of cards, flashlights, dead batteries by the tens and twenties; black bugs dead and alive; lobster pots, a soup ladle, muffin tins, pot holders burnt at the edges; broken dishes intended for repair set in a pile with a tube of dried-up epoxy on top; a magazine in Spanish with a picture of Frank Sinatra on the cover; misfolded maps of Romania, Chile, and New Mexico, and a road atlas of the U.S. with most of the states torn out; board games broken up like driftwood—Monopoly, Risk, and Clue—sets of Chinese checkers, backgammon, dominoes and chess; piles of *Reader's Digest* dog-eared; the *Farmer's Almanac* from 1963–68; newspaper clippings—MOONWALK, KENNEDY'S DEAD, NIXON RESIGNS, and her father's obituary from 1984 in lowercase; old fishing licenses and regulations for herself, her brothers, sisters-in-law, her father and mother, and people whose names she did not recognize, all alphabetized in a recipe index file with a rubber band around the whole; more dead bugs; a stuffed fish taken from one of the oceans and chewed by mice; a small pine box from the five-and-dime in town with the name of the Lake in gold cursive on top and someone's rock collection inside; a marriage license with names smeared; a box of push pins.

She didn't remember where any of it came from.

Once Ruth had fished one of his blue-lipped twins from the bottom of Clay Bay. She dove and got the twin. She swam and pulled the twin. She coughed and dragged the twin. She kicked and lifted the twin. She twitched and breathed for the twin. Skin to skin, lip to lip, tongue to tongue. He had penned and posted the letter five days later.

Jim and his wife moved to Hawaii and sold the cottage. They were all old people by then. The wife had picked Hawaii. Nothing could be completely clearer.

5. Don't plunge into cold water when exhausted or overheated.

She swam out and out. The crawl proper, as her father taught her, the breaststroke, then the dog paddle as she tired looking for Victory. She floated on her back to rest. Shore seemed a mile between her toes. She turned and turned. Her legs twisted. Where is Victory? She sank, determined to find bottom, but her feet never touched and she pulled at water to get back to air. She treaded, the most efficient form of staying alive, then tucked under again to spin and search the water with open eyes. Where's the rock?

"A rock that big does not just depart unannounced from a lake."

"No. It's considered rude."

"Father?"

"But if a rock does depart unexpectedly, the swimmer should wait patiently for its return."

"Is that the next instruction?"

"Yes."

She treaded and turned, treaded and turned.

She did not completely believe in telepathy anymore. She didn't think she believed in *completely* anymore. A dive for a twin was only reflex. The loons were rarely saved.

Ruth's best friend was Elsa for years. Elsa was German and once had a dog she'd stolen, kidnapped from some substandard people at the foot of the Lake. The dog had been shaved and its hair dyed from blond to brown after the theft to prevent detection, identification, and all subsequent injustice. Ruth admired Elsa very much.

6. Don't get panicky when in danger.
She floated. She counted the cabins on shore and lost count at three. She knew it was the wrong number except in case of fire, panic, or dynamite, which can kill even the most enormous rock, anything, a hill, a mountain. A big enough bird could pluck the rock from the Lake and away, a mistaken mouse, anything at all is possible with the right size talons. A mere rock stands no chance, a girl child.
She went under for the first time.

Smug. The thing with him was. If she had to say.

She once talked to him, mouth-to-ear, on the cot in her screen porch. Sound carried so far over calm water.

"A rock as big as Victory Rock must have been deposited by a glacier during the retreat of the last Ice Age."

"Fascinating," he said. They were playing with each other's private parts.

"It's known as an erratic," she said kissing his nose sweetly.

"I like that word," he said with enthusiasm.

"All those other stones are from the glacier too," she said. "The small ones everywhere on the bottom and shore. Even the tiniest ones."

"Who cares about them," he said, annoyed.

"Do you get it?"

"Yes."

"It's out of place," she said. "That's why erratic. See?"

"Yes. Come here."

"Out of scale."

"Yes. I get it."

"Completely out of scale."

"Yes."

She bobbed up and breathed once. Then she went down the second time. All swimmers will bob up a third time.

At night, with her eyes shut, she had chipped away at the rock until it was a pile of pebbles, practically sand, small enough for the fish to eat it by mistake.

The dog barked somewhere.

It was probably Elsa's dog off its tether again roaming the beach. She liked that dog. Elsa's place was so near the road, dangerous to animals. She might look for it later. Tie it up. Down the steps to the dock to the canoe to the beach.

Blue Nevus

Preamble to the National Space Agency Employee Manual
1. Safety first.

"Hey, Roger, what the hell is that blue thing on your arm?" said Stan Penrod in Locker Room One. He was zipping his old NSA jumpsuit, which was too tight for him.

"Hey, Roger Cotton. Hey, men. Come look at Roger Cotton's arm. There's something on it."

The men stopped dressing and undressing.

Stan Penrod's voice had military training. That was part of it. Although retired, Stan Penrod's voice was still like the tip of a missile, a fact that cannot be discounted here. Or at least noted. Stan had been short-listed for the Ulysses Program in the middle of that century. The body ages at a particular rate, but the trained voice declines more slowly. Modern medicine has noted this.

"My God," Stan's voice beaconed more softly. "It's like a little blue caterpillar walking on dough."

The naked men and half-dressed men and men in towels on the edge of the cloud of steam which billowed from the shower entrance turned. They looked at Roger Cotton on Bench 6, slumped and gray with his clasped hands. Though Stan Penrod is tangential to the story at best, peripheral at best, a distraction.

"Hey, Roger, that blue thing looks very bad," said Stan and waved his cigar.

The men of the Y gathered closer around Roger Cotton's biceps, breathing in Stan's smoke. The cigar was a violation, of course, but who was going to stop Stan Penrod?

Roger Cotton leaned on a tower of clean, white towels just delivered to the bench by gloved staff.

"It's nothing," said Roger Cotton. He covered the blue thing with his hand.

"Looks like cancer," said Alonzo Porter in his racquetball gear.

This was back when everyone died of it. The towels fell. The buzzer sounded. Men looked at the clock above the door and hurried with their things. They ran off to the pool, the weight room, the Jacuzzi tub.

"I'm late," said Stan Penrod. He took up his racquetball gear. "Have that thing looked at, Roger."

Stan Penrod exited the swinging door to Locker Room One. He crushed out the cigar in the water fountain on his way. The few remaining men rewrapped their towels.

"It's only a Blue Nevus," Roger said to the lockers. "I've had it checked out."

"Never heard of it," said Alonzo Porter at the drinking fountain, a baritone.

"It's well known and totally benign," said Roger Cotton. "A Blue Nevus is naturally occurring, nothing at all. The doctors said so."

"Doctors," said Alonzo. He disappeared into steam.

"But blue is not a color the skin should make," said Max Robinson, a minister, who would live to be one hundred and fifty-two. "It's a worry. Remember, cancer is also naturally occurring."

"Yes, that's right," someone said.

"And Ebola is naturally occurring too," said Alonzo, who

had forgotten his shampoo. "There have been outbreaks in South America moving northward."

"I need water," said Roger Cotton.

Albert Bunting filled a Dixie Cup and handed it to Roger. Roger drank. The men watched his Adam's apple go. The men lost interest. The last of them took showers or talked of other things or went away.

"What's Martha say about this blue thing?" said Albert Bunting. They sat on Bench 6 and leaned on their knees.

"Martha's in Omaha," said Roger.

"I see," said Albert Bunting, who had a cold and blew his nose. "Pardon me."

"Thank you for being kind," said Roger Cotton. "They promoted her to oxygen washers. Omaha is the epicenter for that research, as you know."

"Of course, of course," said Albert Bunting and he draped a towel over Roger's arm like a cape. "Well, I'm glad you're starting tennis."

Roger Cotton nodded, "Yes, me too. It relaxes the mind. I've also been doing yard work, raking and pruning."

Albert Bunting took a shower. Roger Cotton sat and waited for the locker room to clear.

When Alonzo Porter dried off, he was looking thin and ill but he and Albert Bunting shaved in the mirrors and had their usual talk: about the recent bicycle thefts in Lennox with no suspects at all, about their frustration with the head master of Lennox Science Academy, they were both on the Board, and about how worrisome it was to see acceptance rates of LSA graduates declining at the Air Force Academy.

"The lifeblood of the school is draining," said Alonzo Porter. "I hate to see the school jeopardized like this." Alonzo spoke in the same gruff tone as always, but the volume was lower, much lower, Roger Cotton noticed as he pretended to read a tennis magazine.

After they rinsed their faces, Alonzo and Albert talked of Kelsey Starr's recent visit for her thirty-sixth birthday. It was her last trip home before the preflight quarantine. They discussed a rumored Kelsey Starr boyfriend.

"I hope it's true," said Albert Bunting. "She deserves happiness."

"She's really taken her sweet time," Alonzo Porter said. "Her eggs are dying. Her mother was getting frantic about it according to Jason."

Roger Cotton listened to their happy talk. Barbecues and invitations. He studied the ceiling, mildewed and cracking. Rebar broke through and the ceiling crumbled down. When the men were gone, Roger Cotton tried his locker, but forgot his combination. The basement of the Y would be renovated soon after and a decade later the Y would be moved to a retrofitted building on Appleton and Markley.

Roger took a shower without soap. The hot water pummeled his shiny head and naked skin just like it would anyone's. Roger Cotton dried off. He drank at the fountain. He found bandages in the bottom of an open locker near Bench 7 and fumbled to cover the Blue Nevus. He dressed. He walked to his car and sat for a long time on the bumper under the parking lot light. It was a terrible car. The Middle Ages was a better time to live. Life spans were shorter and more defined. Smallpox and Black Plague took people quickly regardless of sin or previous health. Horses were the main form of transportation, besides walking, which was what most people did, the average people. Average horses lived and died and had average foals who lived and died. The people fed the horses in the fields. The people opened the fence door and watched

the horses walk through. Once upon a time, people brushed
horses in the morning as their first act of the day. They picked
the dirt between the horse's shoes at noon. The horses stood
and ate in beautifully green fields in the afternoon. It was a
wonderful time.

A child's small bike leaned unchained on the fence. It
was an older model, green and yellow, with streamers and a
bell. It had a flat tire. The child had left the bike stranded
and gone to get help. But this child had not found help. This
child had not returned. Once upon a time, there were people
down the street such as cobblers and blacksmiths who could
fix the bike in a snap and who cared about the child, who
wanted to make his life good, who asked after his happiness
and well-being amongst themselves.

Roger looked around him. The parking lot was empty.
The Y lights were still on but it was just the janitor. A car was
parked on Campbell with its interior lights on, but no one
was in it. Roger waved at the car to be sure. No one waved
back. Roger opened his trunk. He went to the bike and petted the green and yellow seat. He picked up the bike by the
throat of the handles and laid the bike in his trunk. The bell
trilled as he slammed the trunk door. Roger Cotton drove
home smelling of Stan Penrod's cigar. He carried the small
bike down the basement steps to the Ping-Pong table, which
was never used anymore for Ping-Pong. He pulled the string
over the net for light.

On the near-court, Roger Cotton stored his collection
of silver and gold amulets, arranged in a small city of boxes
within the service line. Across the net in the far-court stood
a corresponding city of boxes, the amalgamated metals, the
coppers and the pewters too, the lesser amulets, neatly lined
and stacked, rarely opened. In total, the entire Ping-Pong

table metropolis was built of one hundred and twenty-seven amulet boxes. Each small, handcrafted trinket within represented the handiwork of one of Roger Cotton's favorite historical and notable human cultures of the extinct past: amulets crafted in celebration of the Golden Age of postcolonial Africa, high-latitude/nonguttural Native American, and the late-north Low Frisian of central Europe were his special subspecialties, though he owned a smattering of others. He had ordered them from Mexico City as he and Martha could afford it. It was a thorough collection, but hardly exhaustive. This was just the beginning. He stood and admired the shadow the tallest buildings cast.

Roger Cotton set the bike down. He rolled it and parked it against the far-court backhand line. Its small front wheel and handlebars tangled easily into the cluster of seventeen other bikes.

That night, Roger shaved his mustache with the straight edge. The bathroom mirror needed cleaning, but that was Martha's work. The mirror had a round face and a round lip. At the doctor's office, there had been a glass box with a phone girl in it with a headset over her skull. She talked to air: dirty carpet, orange plastic chairs, old magazines. The hairs over Roger's lip were like dried-up grass. The doctor was dark and smelled of carpets and frankincense from India or Mongolia but the diploma said Baltimore. Roger had looked at the diploma closely. He had taken it from the wall and cleaned it with his sleeve while waiting for this doctor forty-three minutes.

A toothpaste lump fell. It stuck to the sink. Roger picked the skin with his nail and the lump slid away. The hairs slid down the drain, gone, absolutely gone.

Roger heard a noise in the house and called "Martha?"

No, it was not Martha. It was the Blue Nevus. Blue Nevus. Blue Nevus.

Roger neatened his sideburns with the straightedge and said something original: Up yours, Cinderella, you pink-pantied Fool, you Glass-shoed liar, what a Moron you are. I wish the stepsisters had burned your Dress. Smashed your Pumpkin. Caught your Mice in a Trap and dropped them in the Barrel, the one in your stepmother's Barn.

He wrote it down then tore it up. He knew he had gone too far.

When done with the sideburns, Roger pressed the blade to the neck of Blue Nevus but did not cut. Everything was backward in the mirror, confusing and dangerous. Roger Cotton went to bed since a good night sleep changes everything.

In the morning, Roger Cotton tried Martha's number in Omaha. He left a message. Before work he wrote a card to Ms. Kelsey Starr. He addressed it to her in Omaha at NSA head-quarters on the Flight Crew Campus, though he knew her to be traveling in Europe on a promotional tour for the Gypsy VIII Program. She would get the card when she returned.

> Dear Kelsey,
> Thanks for the article. I am ever honored you take the time to edify fellow Lennoxonians and your fans. I love your work on meteors, especially, and cancer treatment. I've seen the protesters in Omaha. But they are fear-mongers and people see through that sort of thing. Don't let thugs like that bother you. They are not worthy of your fear. Threats are easy, words, words, words. Enclosed is an interesting article on free-test inversions, my specialty. It might interest you. The best of everything to you. The launch is coming soon, I know, and you must be very, very busy. Please know what an inspiration you are to me and my wife (Martha), who is a colleague of yours over at the Research Pod on NSA campus. She's redesigning

the individual oxygen gooseneck scrubber valve assembly for safety improvements. She's brilliant and always wanted to go up there to space. Like all of us did/do. We can't all go. Maybe you will see her. Say hello from me if you do see her, thanks.

Yours,

Roger Cotton

It was not his place to ask about a new boyfriend. He mailed the card, a pussy willow print signifying spring, on his way to work. That day, work scheduled Roger for six Marksman inverter installations, laborious and tedious. He was running nonstop from nine to five though hardly at the top of his game. His Blue Nevus was throbbing.

National Space Risk Assessment Manual
1. Safety first.
2. Space is not political.

Kelsey Starr got her foot in the door during the Gypsy VI era when most in Lennox had lost hope. Lennox worried, by then, Kelsey was wasting her time. Other flight candidates from various Tier One institutions could match Kelsey Starr's skill set; they were younger, and they did not carry with them the "always the bridesmaid" aura. But Kelsey Starr made the alternate list a month before the last launch of Gypsy VI. The destination was a rendezvous off Titan with a meteor field of particular promise for Uranium 238 harvest, one of Kelsey Starr's subspecialties. When a fluke flu hit Omaha and knocked out the meteoric science officer three days before launch, Jason Starr was the only person not surprised. He said privately that his daughter was like an old-style caboose: "Never first on board, often last, but Kelsey always made it on the train."

Kelsey proved herself on Gypsy VI and VII, and by VIII there was no question who would fill the science officer slot for important meteor work. Kelsey was also well liked. She was outstanding with crowds and children and the press. Protesters' accusations of corruption and incompetence at NSA, criticism of privatization of public resources for the gains of big mining interests, and general attacks on the imperialistic nature of space travel were rendered impotent by Kelsey Starr's open, forthright, scientific style and small town manners. Everyone loved her. Kelsey Starr was brilliant, competent, and good for crew morale on the torturously long round trips to the frontier mineral outposts that obsessed the NSA at the time. She was a shrewd staffing decision from the upper levels of the Gypsy VIII Program, despite all its other well-known disappointments.

The Gypsy VIII was the most perfected class of craft of its day. Designers and engineers had worked out all the persistent issues with deep cold solubility and permeability that had plagued previous versions of the craft. Kelsey Starr, at the time, was still a middle-30s tomboy. She did five hundred sit-ups a day, but was not beefy. She drank only persimmon tea and water and gave up all meats native to her upbringing due to current damning analysis of nitrates and the liver. Kelsey had a pristine liver. She had perfect organs generally, as preflight body scans and development scans for the CODE premortem cloning system confirmed. She was, in fact, the favored subject of all the CODE scientists since all her organs ranked in the ninety-ninth percentile. Kelsey Starr had a lifespan expectation range from one hundred and ten years on the low end to one hundred and twenty-eight years on the high depending, of course, on lack of unforeseen mishap, unnatural death, foul play, or inadvertent toxicity exposures. She looked twenty-five at the blastoff of Gypsy VIII.

"I think they're wrong," she told the reporter for a women's magazine. "I expect to live to be one hundred and forty-eight." Kelsey Starr had a disarming, nonprofessional voice.

"How does that feel?" a magazine asked.

"It feels like I am the luckiest person on planet Earth," Kelsey Starr said.

"Do you have hobbies?"

"Horseback riding."

"Do you have a boyfriend, Ms. Starr? We've heard rumors."

"No comment."

"Some people criticize the space program for unethical practices. You yourself, we understand, have received death threats. What do you say to those people, Ms. Starr?"

"Space is not political," Kelsey said.

"That's a slogan, Ms. Starr," said the magazine.

"Space is personal," said Kelsey. "We are all all alone just like that."

"How tall are you anyway?"

"6'1"."

"That's very tall for space travel."

"Yes," she smiled. "It certainly is."

The suit Kelsey designed as a post-doc altered the field. She spoke to her mother on Saturdays at 9 AM unless in a different time zone. She wrote weekly longhand to her father. She braided her hair daily. The tail touched her coccyx and drew cameras even before becoming an alternate. She had attended Lennox Public High School though accepted to the Academy, and had been the high school mascot in a brown fuzzy suit. The buck-toothed head was separate, clawed feet and a flat slapping tail—the Lennox Fighting Beaver with a braid down its back. SMALL TOWN BEAVER BLASTS OFF was printed in a font that had not been used by the *Lennox News* since a 20th-century president was shot.

In the Christmas parade, Kelsey Starr had her own float. Roy's Service built it with sheet metal, a capsule over the bucket of his loader, in which she sat and waved when home for the holidays. "HITCH YOUR WAGON TO A STARR!" one banner read and was rolled up later and stored in the basement under the Ping-Pong table the rest of the year. Martha never liked her.

"All flash," Martha said, and never attended the parade. Such factors must be measured and calculated, if possible, for an understanding of the beginning.

At high school commencement, Kelsey Starr spoke as valedictorian. It was a humble speech about small towns and lifelong friendship.

"May we all live exciting, happy, successful lives," she said, concluding her speech. "May we all love everyone!"

She sat on the stage after. A man in a mustache brought her a glass of water while the superintendent stood at the podium to gave his statement that concluded in the following:

> Remember this, graduates: A beaver was once like a mermaid in water, turning and diving for pure joy. She slapped her tail at strangers, yes, but only to make her territory clear. She was nature's perfect creature of industry. Beavers never gave up, were never greedy, or complained. (My mother, in fact, once saw an actual beaver in an old national park.) A beaver took what she needed only. She helped others when possible. If the dam of another was destroyed by flood or incursion, she would hurry and swim to help stem the flow. Her teeth never stopped growing. It was her nature to chew and build. Her bloody spittle was left on forest stumps and *calcified there* for decades. A beaver became intimately close to few, biologists say,

though she was kind to all, and she loved lodge and family. She was a wonderful species and hope persists with continuing Canadian efforts at repopulation. May your generation continue to attend to the world's most vexing and persistent problems, like the beaver, with wonderful progress.

But, graduates, remember this also as you strike your path tonight. The beaver was brave and a fine swimmer. She was an example to follow *in her aquatic life*. But if a beaver found herself too far from lake or lodge, she, being shy and slow on land, was easily caught by unfriendly predatory jaws, even merely thoughtlessly or unseeing, who can say why? Thus, she might easily be snagged in a leg-trap to be skinned out and flayed out by any bungler. My friends, take note of the beaver. Keep close to your safe shores. Good luck to you.

The kids threw their caps in the air. They knew exactly what the superintendent meant. It was an old speech. He had used it for the class of '35 and some of the graduates had siblings in that class so had heard it before. The kids collected the caps between the folding chairs and divvied them up. Some heads did not fit. It hardly mattered. "Moments like this are important!" the superintendent called over their heads and caps as the kids headed for the swimming hole at the old gravel pit for the celebration.

National Space Assessment Checklist Manual Preamble
1. Checklist is order.
2. Order is safety.

On the way to Alonzo Porter's Celebration of Life, Roger Cotton's car broke down. He pushed the car under a big tree on Cherry. He waited for the tow. He wrote a note for the tow driver to leave on the dash:

Hello Roy—I hope things are good on your end. My
car has some very serious sounding/seeming problems.
It was making a terrible sound under the engine and
rattling. Started overheating very suddenly (smoking)
and the battery and brake lights came on. I was afraid
to drive it, then it died. Can you work on it? I'm at
BN-672321, as always. Talk to you soon about this,
I hope. Sincerely,
Roger Cotton.
PS: I'm having some other troubles right now (with
my skin and a recent loss of a friend). It would be outstanding if you could get this car worked up promptly.
Martha sends her best. (Key in ignition.)

The tow dropped Roger off at Alonzo Porter's curb. The
rooms were full of mourners shocked by Alonzo's sudden
death. The air was warm with cheese and meat. The dining
table was scattered with bowls and crocks and the spoons la-
beled up the shaft with masking tape.

"If he'd been in Africa, or an African, we would have
burned him on a pyre with some colorful robes, the chief of
a tribe, a king, a man of resource," they toasted. They sang
songs to a picture of Alonzo on an easel. The casseroles were
abundant: lidded in circles, ovals, squares and rectangles.
Steam squeezed from their lips. The women wore mitts and
aprons and flew by like comets with flowers. Roger held the
kitchen door open with his back. He held his arm as if in a
sling.

"How's that arm?" said Albert Bunting the way a brother
or uncle might speak.

"The doctors took it off," said Roger Cotton. "The Blue
Nevus."

"I'm glad to hear it," said Albert Bunting. "Will you
have a scar?"

"Not much of one," said Roger Cotton.

"The right diagnosis is everything," said Albert Bunting, and waved at Jonelle Porter who was weeping near the arctic entry. "Who's your doctor?"

Roger Cotton said the name of the doctor.

"I met that doctor once," said Albert Bunting. "A dark man and foreign. I have nothing against that. That doctor won the city tennis tournament, the whole damn thing, the first year he entered. Where do you think this doctor learned tennis?"

"I don't know," said Roger Cotton. "I have no idea at all."

"I feel badly about Alonzo," Albert Bunting said. "But it was quick and natural. Cavemen just died like that too. With spears and rock rings on the top of a blue sky hill."

"I know it," said Roger Cotton.

"It's admirable," said Albert Bunting. "Most death is common."

Roger Cotton drank down his juice and seltzer from a plastic cup while Albert Bunting had real glass. Alonzo's urn was on the mantle between two sets of Dutch figurines dancing. Jonelle Porter wore high heels. There was a lump in the carpet runner to the kitchen and Roger Cotton bent and pressed at the lump in the carpet. Albert Bunting looked healthy.

"You look very healthy," said Roger Cotton.

"Omaha has a wonderful layout," said Albert Bunting later. He set his plate on a plate on the table. Max Robinson passed by picking his neck. "Wonderful brickwork and history."

"Yes," said Roger Cotton.

"Omaha has a wonderful zoo," said Albert Bunting.

"Martha likes animals so much," said Roger Cotton.

"Lennox is sunnier than Omaha," said Albert Bunting "You should remind Martha that Lennox is sunny."

"Oh, I will," said Roger Cotton.

Stan Penrod arrived. Roger Cotton found his umbrella and departed. He walked from street to street looking for his car. The sun set. Walking home, Roger found a bike abandoned between a fire hydrant and a tree. It was unlocked and not tethered in the smallest way. Roger Cotton had no brothers or uncles. He took the bike.

He rode the bike the whole way home seven blocks north and seven blocks west.

At night, the Blue Nevus moved over his body. From the biceps to the shoulder was the usual. But sometimes the Blue Nevus moved in the ear and crossed to the other shoulder. The Blue Nevus roved him.

Roger Cotton roved the house, which was an average wood house. He cleaned the mirrors. He called Martha and left a message. He cleaned the ice trays. He roved again, entering and exiting the rooms of the house through various hatches with knobs.

"They are doors," Roger Cotton said. "These hatches are only doors."

He pulled the doors closed behind him by way of the knobs. He climbed the stairs that were covered with carpet and silent in slippers. In the second floor ceiling, one door pulled down with a loop on a string and a staircase lowered. It was an average wood stairway. It was narrow and steep.

"It is only a stairway," said Roger Cotton holding the stairway.

He climbed up the stairway to the attic. "It is only an attic," he said and sat in the dusty rocking chair by a pair of skis.

From the rocking chair, he scanned the moons and planets for their peculiar movements through a small paned window. He set the skis across his knees as a tippy writing table.

Roger Cotton rubbed his arm. He looked through the glass at the black sky: if this was not the rocking chair in the attic but the commander's chair of the Omaha Control Capsule Simulator, for example, the capsule exit hatch would, of course, sit just up between those rafters. The exit hatch would open by way of a loop on string and a staircase would lower: a steel amalgam weighing no more than regulation: twenty kilos. In such a case, Roger Cotton would climb up the second stairway to the Gypsy VIII Observation Deck, the real one, not some Nebraska simulation. Kesley Starr would be there setting up her experiments, she was so diligent. On the Observation Deck, the rows of oscilloscopes would line up and whine, scanning for white giants and red dwarfs in the bay windows in the nose of the craft, which would, in such a case, most likely be tethered to the proboscis of the newest, most colossal orbiting dock tower. How wonderful. A batch of asteroids would fly by.

"Perfectly Beautiful," Roger Cotton wrote in the crew log, a dusty book from the floor. He watched the sky for additional facts. Check.

If so.

Dead-center in the dome of the Observation Deck would sit the sky-exit hatch made of thinnest ultrapress, the latest. Roger Cotton's ancestors had been tall people and he set the crew log and the skis aside and stood. He went to the old oak armoire in the corner of the attic for his suit. As always, his fingers found the suit in the dark by way of the old leather and ruff at the collar. How his fingers loved skin and fur. Roger Cotton pulled on the old suit: one arm then the other arm. The arms were snug. The arms were too short, his ancestors had been thin-armed, short-armed people, though tall. The skirts of the suit hung to the floor. He secured the button at his collar and the sash, velvet, the silver epaulets on the shoulder, fringe. Check. Ready?

"Affirmative. Over."

He sat back down in the rocking chair. He reset the skis. He reopened the crew log on the leather and farthest buttons.

If so, if so.

After forty-five-second decompression, the sky-exit hatch would open by way of a loop on string and a staircase would lower, polished steelene. Roger Cotton would climb up the staircase in his spacesuit for a prescheduled spacewalk. He would have been preassigned by the higher ups for a *human-only* assessment and level B checklist. He would bounce up the staircase. Happy. Check.

"I'm ascending to the sky-exit hatch. Over."

He would squeeze out the hatch with his harness and O_2 tether dragging, and secure the hatch with the knuckle peg. Glide out. Swim out. Float out, Roger Cotton. Check.

"Spacewalk commencement underway. Over."

"We have you on the screen. Over."

Roger Cotton turned to a new page in the log. The further instructions:

Turn about and see:
(1) noting peculiar pulsars present, check.
(2) noting errant nevi lingering and loitering, check.
(3) initiating and confirming daily waste ejection procedure. Activating shoulder joint assembly, check. The shoulder socket unscrews, check. The flanges expand from the biceps and releases, check, check. The arm is jettisoned, check.

"The Blue Nevus is jettisoned. Over."

"Roger that, Commander. Over."

The skis fell and frightened the cat. The rocker nearly crushed its tail, but no, the tail flew through to safety: just barely, though such factors as regulation guidelines and feline appendages often *corresponded by coincidence* with critical but unrelated other factors, a particularly vulnerable moment in the case history, for example, some crushing other moment, and cannot be discounted ever, if sequence and consequence are to be uniquely understood.

From the rocking chair, Roger Cotton requested a private transmission to Omaha: "Martha, I want to be with you. Over." It was forever unclear if Martha received the message. Solar storms were at their zenith that night, always a nuisance in that season, causing catastrophic radio interferences all around the star system.

The morning after the Alonzo Turner's Celebration of Life, Roger called Dr. Frankincense. The Physician's Pavilion was downtown. The receptionist on the phone said she could squeeze Roger Cotton in at one. Could he make that time slot? She had a cloying, sycophantic, disgusting voice.

"Yes, I can," Roger Cotton said.

Next, Roger Cotton called Roy's Service to check on his car and left a message.

The doctor's pen was tied to a clipboard with a string. A hole was cut in the glass for the receptionist to talk through. This pen practice was so common as to seem trite. Roger Cotton signed in.

This receptionist was mostly likely a former patient. She had a sizable strawberry scar on one side of her face. It was the color of boiling jam.

"Staring is rude," the receptionist said.

Roger Cotton slid the clipboard through the hole in the glass then sat down in an orange plastic chair. This receptionist was stamping files, *thud thud*, noises like a heavy animal walking from a swampy area into dark leaning trees.

The cavemen could smell such a beast from five miles. The prehistorical wind would carry the scent of game that far while the hungry caveman's olfactory glands were pristine, untarnished by the abuses of modern chemistry, and second to none. The caveman sharpened his spear. He walked across the savanna, through tall grasses, crossed the cold river up to his shins smelling the blood of his prey. He plunged up the hill, which warmed his blood.

"Staring is very rude," said the receptionist. She snapped a blue-green bubble at Roger Cotton, like a monster in an old story.

Once upon a time the orange plastic chair was tangerine. It was hard and his legs slipped. Roger Cotton read about the meteor protests in Omaha and at other major centers, Honolulu, Houston, and Akron, where threats had become actual, delivered in mock meteor bombs. Roger Cotton moved to another plastic chair.

"The doctor will see you now," said the nurse at the door. Roger stood and set down the magazine.

Kelsey Starr's dissertation at Cal Poly made waves in academia. "Gravity: Newton's Miscalculation" was understood by almost no one in Lennox except her father, a physics professor at the university. It's true, Jason Starr was old school. He did quibble over her details and several conclusions. They did argue at the kitchen table but Jason Starr was proud. When Kelsey made Gypsy VI, he passed the Newton paper around amongst his circle: men of the Lennox Science Academy Board, university science department heads, and other select people.

Other copies of the Newton paper did, somehow, get out to the public and circulate. It was public record, after all, and people were fascinated by the new Lennox star in all her variety.

"I didn't get past the first sentence," said most average readers in Lennox coffee shops and Laundromats.

Roger Cotton found his copy on the bench at the Y. He understood every word and had no quibbles whatsoever.

"Not one quibble? Not a single quibble? No, no because Roger Cotton doesn't quibble."

"Stop it, Martha, don't."

"Roger won't quibble."

"Martha, give it back."

> Dear Kelsey,
> Thanks for the check-in. Europe sounds wonderful. I'm well though I have some sad problems right now you might understand. I don't want to burden you, but I have a request.

National Space Agency Code of Conduct
1. Respect and Dignity
2. Infractions
3. Violations
4. Penalties

"I can't live with this arm," Roger said to Dr. Frankincense.

"As I've said, Blue Nevi are harmless," said the doctor. "I have one myself."

The doctor tapped his knee. He spoke exactly like an American, brave-sounding, articulate, and confident.

"I want it off," said Roger. "That's all. I must have it off. I'm losing sleep over it."

The doctor buzzed the nurse who rolled in a tray of tools.

"I hope it's not too late," Roger Cotton added.

The nurse prepared the Blue Nevus with a cotton ball. She gave an injection at an angle near its mouth, a long needle and only briefly painful. The nurse and Dr. Frankincense wore masks, gloves, and lights on their heads. The goggles were huge and clean. The scalpel slipped in. The blade cut an oblong ring around the Blue Nevus.

"There is nothing to worry about," said Dr. Frankincense.

There was very little blood. The gloved hands were swift and neat. The nurse handed in tweezers and a tiny tool that worked like a spatula.

"My wife is in Omaha now," said Roger Cotton. "She could not get away for my procedure."

"It's really and truly unnecessary," said the doctor. The needle crossed with black thread trailing. The skin sucked shut. In the end, the Blue Nevus sat on the gauze on the tray in its own yellow ooze. The doctor snapped off his gloves and exited.

"I dislike doctors," said Roger to the nurse when the door shut.

"No one likes to come to the doctor," she muttered. She had braces on her teeth that affected her pronunciation. She was pretty in a plain way, like most people, when she smiled.

"What will they do with my Blue Nevus now?"

"They'll send it to Kansas City to the medical incinerator."

"But I'd like it to do some good," said Roger. "After all this trouble and misery. Maybe something memorable."

"Incineration is the rule," the nurse said.

"I'd like my Blue Nevus to serve science somehow," he said. He followed the nurse and the rolling tray into the hall.

"I know what you mean," she said and touched his good arm. "No laboratories are studying Blue Nevi at this time. They are not significant." She pushed the cart away.

At the glass box, Roger Cotton showed his Health Card to the receptionist.

"Sign here," she said and he signed.

"We will see you on the thirteenth, Mr. Cotton," she said, not unfriendly now, and wrote out a card with the date. She gave him the card through the hole in the glass. He might have exited then. Instead Roger Cotton bent his mouth to the hole in the glass.

"You are the ugliest person I've ever seen," he said to her.

That night, the Blue Nevus stitches itched and burned. He tried not to scratch them, as Martha always said not to. But in the end he disobeyed her. He pulled the gauze off. He scratched. In the dark under the covers it was soothing at first.

He dabbed cream on the stitches in the bathroom. In the tool room he found a fresh straight-edge pack and cut a wider ring around the stitches. In the hall mirror, he excised the blue tissue the doctor had missed. It was a painful procedure, but life is painful. At the end of the procedure, the stitches floated like a black island in a capillary sea. He stored the Blue Nevus excess in a silver amulet of Navajo design, one of his favorite of the collection. He set the amulet in the basement freezer.

Roy's Service sat between the new dump and an out-of-business modern dance studio at what was then the outskirts of Lennox. Martha had gone to high school with Roy. That was the only connection. Since their marriage, no one had touched Roger and Martha's car but Roy. Roy's shop was on the bus route.

"WE FIX ANYTHING" was painted on the belly of an old-style cement truck. It stood on a rotating platform at the center of the yard. Junkers were clustered under the cement truck like ducklings. The belly turned counterclockwise one rotation hourly while the platform rotated hourly clockwise, each 8760 rotations per year, assuming no malfunctions. The cement truck was a famous Lennox landmark.

Roy's shop was open-air in summer. Tools of every kind were in plain view to passersby or from the bus: drills, presses, power-hammers and welders and the universe of saws: hack saws, wet saws, circular saws, duplicating saws, jig saws were all there for the taking. Lennox was a trusting town. Kelsey Starr kept her Phoenix Speedster under a canvas tarp at Roy's. Roy kept it tuned and ready for when Kelsey was home.

"Your car's not finished yet," said Roy to Roger Cotton in his greasy voice. He wiped his hands on a dirty rag. "It has a mysterious problem. What's wrong with your arm?"

"Just a sprain," said Roger and he lifted the sling. "I'm off work right now."

"Oh," said Roy. "Hi to Martha."

Roger Cotton took the bus home. His arm throbbed. He set the sling on the bus sill. The window was cracked and wind cooled the sling. Lennox flew by. These nights, when the route was ended, Roger got off at the station at midnight. He walked home from streetlight to streetlight. He sometimes stood in the dark cusps between the streetlights and went missing from the universe.

Weeks passed.

While on sick leave, Roger took the intercity bus to Omaha that departed three times daily. Tickets at the zoo were priced so that anyone could go. The motto of the zoo was "Animals Are For Everyone!" There was a sliding scale. The bus and zoo had a promotional partnership. The bus lurched at stops, yes, but there was no reason to have a car.

The ride took three hours. On the way, Roger Cotton called Martha and left a message. He collected and sorted the coupons printed on the old bus tickets found on the floor.

Some were found under the seats and in the men's room in the station. A free bag of animal crackers was often offered but for some animals only, the petting zoo, for example, with the camels at your own risk. The parrots at the entrance were given so many they were never hungry. Roger Cotton looked for her there at every cage. The monkeys licked themselves and others. The lions licked themselves and others. The zebras licked themselves and others. Roger loved the savanna best, an acre and a quarter, the biggest in the Midwest, old prairie grass reseeded. From the gift shop window he watched the protesters who were truly everywhere with their pickets and sit-ins. They stomped and sang. He thought of joining and lighting a candle to a dead baby elephant they'd stuffed and mounted on the protest flatbed. It was parked in the loading zone.

The perforations on the coupons were often pristine. At home, Roger Cotton kept the perfect perforations in a pile by the flour jar until the expiration dates. After two months, Roy sold the car for parts since the vehicle could not be fixed. He sent Roger Cotton the money in the mail. Upon receipt of the check, which said WE FIX ANYTHING at the top center, Roger climbed up into the attic, sat in the rocker, and wrote in the crew log: Up yours, Roy Martin, you grease-fingered Liar, you foul-toothed Ape, what a Charlatan you are. Mr. Genius: so you do Trig in your head? Can you feed the Starving on the Starving continents? Water the Droughted? Wive the wifeless? Since ANYTHING means EVERYTHING, Roy. May the Hair-Lipped children hunt you. May the Amputees roast you on a slow turning Spit. Ten thousand turns. Baste you in oil from your Second-Rate Drums.

Roger Cotton was not satisfied with the work, but dated the entry.

"Hello, this is Roger Cotton. I need an appointment to see the doctor as soon as possible. I'm having some issues with my hands."

When Roger Cotton arrived home each night, he raked the bushes and brambles behind his house. Because there was no fence. Because there were no horses to eat the leaves. He arranged the leaves in patterns for Martha.

Blue
Blue Nevus
Blue Nevus Blue Nevus

Then the wind blew the pyramid away. Days passed that seemed like weeks.

"I need to show this hand to the doctor," Roger Cotton said to the receptionist. The hand was wrapped in gauze and taped.

"He's with a patient," said the receptionist.

"This concerns him," said Roger Cotton. "This situation is relevant to his future."

The receptionist buzzed the nurse who unwrapped the gauze and saw the stump of the pinkie and buzzed the doctor. The doctor entered and closed the door.

"Please sit down," Roger Cotton said. The doctor sat. Roger Cotton gave the doctor the hand.

"What have you done?" said the doctor. "You've butchered your finger."

"It had Blue Nevus spreading everywhere," said Roger Cotton holding the stump. "I value my fingers, yes, of course, but I want to live."

Roger Cotton rolled the tool cart closer.

"The Blue Nevus is spreading."

"I think you should talk to someone," said the doctor.

Roger Cotton twisted off the iodine cap with his good hand.

"I took the bus here," said Roger Cotton. "I don't have all day."

"I'm sorry, but I can't help you," said the doctor under the wall of diplomas. "I'm not afraid of you, sir."

That night, Roger raked leaves with his good arm. He held a powerful flashlight under the sling. The woods were thick as he cleared the leaves away from under and between and within the branches of the shrubs. The shrubs moved deeper in the unending woods. Roger throbbed in the sling. The woods smelled of clove or cinnamon.

Very late, in the trees, Roger Cotton found Stan Penrod in the woods on a gurney. He was alone and miserable. He was on his back strapped down to a gurney with only his head free to move. Roger Cotton shined the flashlight and Stan called out for help in that highly trained voice. Then the voice changed to a scream and Stan Penrod thrashed and the gurney bucked in the flashlight beam.

"Get that light out of my eyes," Stan snarled.

He was in his pajamas with the top unbuttoned. His chest was open to the air. In a hole in Stan's belly a medical fixture was drilled into the skin and fitted with a steel ring. The hole was smoking like a tiny dormant volcano. The whole assembly was an inch left of the belly button, rising and falling as Stan breathed. The steel ring would fit a cigarette or cigar perfectly.

Roger held the flashlight to his face. "It's me Roger. What are you doing here?"

"What's it look like?" said Stan, thrashing and thumping with his head. The gurney rattled.

"I don't know," said Roger. "It's confusing to see you."

Stan growled and gnashed. "Give me a cigar," Stan said. "I need one or I'll die. Be a pal."

"I don't have one, I don't smoke," said Roger Cotton. "It's late."

"Give me one or I'll kill you." Stan thrashed. His head pounded the gurney. The rake fell.

"I won't," said Roger. "Settle down. Be quiet."

"I'll settle down if you give me a cigar. I'll be content forever. I don't have all day."

Roger found a cigar in the leaves, then lit the match. The cigar fit snuggly in the steel fitting. The rain began on the trees around the clearing. Stan Penrod relaxed. His belly rose and fell as the smoke swirled down the shaft and in. The ashes drifted off. It was a beautifully quiet time for the two friends.

"Are you happy?"

"Yes, yes," said Stan Penrod.

When Stan started up again, Roger ran home. He went back in the morning for the flashlight and rake.

> Dear Kelsey,
> Thanks for your concern. It's true, installations have become impossible. There was talk of permanent disability and workman's compensation investigations given my exposure to various on-the-job chemicals. I'm skeptical. I'm sure I'll be fine. I have friends and support.

At home Roger Cotton watched reruns of *Beyond Peacocks*, formerly Martha's favorite show. He didn't know what she liked now. "Animals are so comforting," she used to say when feeling low, and Roger Cotton felt this keenly now. Once, before the launch, a pair of young brother giraffes came for dinner. They sat with their legs tucked in the living room and lay their necks along the carpet to the dining room table.

"This is a nice house," said the first in the voice of a girl giraffe. His brother's voice was much lower and stronger.

"Very nice," said the second, who asked Roger about his wife's whereabouts. "Will we meet her this evening too?"

"Shush," said the first.

"No, no, it's fine really," said Roger. "My wife is in Omaha. She works there."

After dinner the brothers went to the yard to stretch and the evening wound down. They ate the trees and then went home.

"I think I'm going mad," Roger Cotton told Albert Bunting soon after. They were in the grocery store line. "I think I'm dying, actually."

"They say if you think you are going mad, it's a sign you can't be," said Albert Bunting. "And you don't look sick. You have good color."

"That's wonderful to hear," said Roger Cotton. "I was getting extremely worried."

National Space Agency Employee Manual
1. Chain of Command
2. Duty and Responsibility

Flowerpots lined the Frankincense driveway at intervals to the bottom steps of the back door. The flowers were exotic and not native to the region. Roger Cotton knocked. The doctor came to the door in his bathrobe. The man's small thin wife hid behind the bathrobe with a steak knife.

"The throbbing is preventing sleep," Roger Cotton said to the doctor in porch light. "I need some more taken off."

"No," said Dr. Frankincense. "You need to leave or I'm calling the police."

The doctor would have closed the door.

"I'm prepared to inform the medical licensing authorities," said Roger Cotton. He waved a paper.

"What is he talking about?" said Mrs. Frankincense. Her husband held the wrist with the knife and whispered in her ear. She whispered back. She rounded her husband. She pulled Roger Cotton into the kitchen. She closed the kitchen door and pulled the blinds. She wiped the table before and after with bleach solution.

> Roger,
> Thanks for the pecans! I love pecans and most nuts! I shared them with the crew. Sounds like life is sort of difficult for you right now. I'm sorry. I hate to hear of people's pain, but I know how that is. HANG IN THERE! They say the pinkie finger will be obsolete in less than fifty thousand years. Chin Up. I hope she comes back home to you soon. My dad knows the mayor of Omaha if you want me to share any of this issue with my trusted family, maybe they can help. They love whoever I love. They are wonderful! That hand sounds terrible. Don't beat yourself up, Roger.
> Best,
> Kesley
> PS: I do accept good luck charms, since you asked. Just nothing over 226 grams, nothing flammable or hazardous. I'd be happy to bring it up there.

Before the space program came to Omaha, the zoo was not much to speak about. But with the space program came a white rhino, a pair of pandas, and funding to build the beloved African savanna at the highest acres of the grounds. There, the lions and zebra roamed free but separated. Zoo designers and biologists were especially proud of the Savanna. It was on the front and center of all brochures, constructed with a tasteful concrete gorge dividing the enclosure in half.

The gorge curved like a river. It ran between the lion's hill and the zebra's hill that had once been the very same hill when the land was prairie. After the space program came, one species could not possibly devour the other.

"Hello, Roger. Roy here. Martha called about the car this week. She's pissed. Maybe you should check with your wife on it. Roy, over and out."

The doctor sent his family to a hotel in Omaha. The doctor stayed to tie up loose ends in Lennox. The house went on the market on August 1. The family moved to Guam in August where his wife had family. Children were born and married in Guam with no trouble. The doctor's practice thrived in Guam. They lived happily there. Lennox grew in the years to come. The population increased such that Lennox was nearly designated an "A2" city for purposes of federal grant funding, which could do such wonders for a community. It was like a dangling carrot. Private exercise clubs were built and the Y diversified. A small civic center was built then expanded to house an orchestra; an amateur opera banded and disbanded. The town forged an affiliation with an outlying prairie park with authentic prairie grass and reproducing herds of buffalo, which failed, and the buffalo were shipped to an up-and-coming park in Wyoming. Some Lennoxonians visited the family in Guam. It is a garden place. The wife did charity work with maimed people, the victims of war in war-torn countries. They changed to her maiden name after six months on the island nation.

> Kelsey,
> I so much want to go to space with you. How can I express it? I've written this essay on Time (enclosed). I'm sending too this amulet and chain. It's near and dear to me and if you don't mind, don't open it. It's

Navaho. I'm just so pleased one small part of me can
go to space, float there. This world is not for me.

In college, Kelsey Starr wrote a short essay entitled "The
Missing Color on the Universal Spectrum," which she used
for her application to Cal Poly, though her father had his
doubts when he heard the subject matter. Belinda rubbed his
back and said, "Don't worry, we raised her right."

"It sounds too philosophical," Jason Starr said. "They
don't go for that way-out stuff at Cal Poly."

"Times change," said Belinda.

As the deadline loomed, Jason Starr tapped on Kelsey's
bedroom door daily to check her progress. As an alum, he
had a stake in it.

"Dad, trust me," said Kelsey. "Go back to bed. I'm thinking this out."

She was still making revisions minutes before the Jan-
uary 1 deadline. Belinda often told friends about this tense
time in their lives.

"We just didn't know," said Belinda.

The essay impressed the readers. Some thought it genius,
some did not understand, but thought it impressive in its "at-
tempting," they said. "This brashness is very rare."

Kelsey Starr was never sick a day in her short life. Once,
Kelsey got a black eye pitching softball, a terrible shiner, but
Kelsey's natural color had returned twenty-nine hours later
after application of a Starr family salve made of arnica, Ep-
som salts, and rosemary. It was later written up by a much
younger cousin as a science fair project.

Once, when Kelsey Starr was in college, she went with her
girlfriends to a fortune teller in Topeka. It was a schoolgirl
lark. The practitioner wore a black beret and had a crystal

ball that she looked into. She said Kelsey Starr would not live to her thirty-seventh birthday. When Kelsey Starr got famous, the fortune teller sold her story. Entire chapters and dissertations have been devoted to the significance of this seemingly small factor. What if, what if? Once upon a time.

National Space Agency Flight Operations Manual
1. Preflight
2. Inflight
3. Postflight
4. CODE Procedures
5. Fraternization Guidelines

The blastoff was routine. Dozens of flower arrangements arrived at Mission Control, cards and letters from kids from her European tour, and packages with trinkets that people hoped might blast off with her and the other crew members. Kelsey took only one: a 224 gram silver amulet, Navajo-styled, sterilized, on a chain zipped up next to her skin under her jumpsuit. The protesters were on hand, of course, with posters and placards. They wore black and the males and females were indistinguishable. Their skin was painted ghoul-ishly like bullet-ridden victims.

"Leave their moons alone," they chanted.

Security had been heightened due to the new CODE installation. The Catastrophic Order for Duplication and Epitomization hardware and software on the Gypsy VIII had never been tested on premortem humans. Up until Gypsy VIII, live mammals had been successfully dupli-cated under the CODE regime with great success from captive populations for repopulation projects all over the redeveloping world. Human cadavers had been used within ten minutes of death but the results were disappointing. It was designed to engage in the last sixty to ninety seconds of life of the subject astronaut in three stages. It had been controversial and expensive, and the naysayers were clamoring to shut the CODE Program down in its infancy. The CODE procedure included: Step 1 was verbal confirmation by the subject astronaut to base ship giving permission to enable the CODE body scan and thereby activate the duplication sequencing switch. Step 2 required the subject astronaut to manually engage the activated sequencing switch under the sliding slot on the left breastplate on her autonomous flight suit to initiate the actual CODE body scan. After the 3.4 second scan was completed, Step 3 required a second verbal confirmation by the subject astronaut of her personal password which, if correct, enabled transmission of two complete sets of blueprints, one to the Duplications Lab in Omaha where the subject astronaut's body would be reconstructed, the other set to the base ship, and a copy sent on by the ship to the Records Room of the Library of Congress in Denver for perpetual open public access and scholarly pursuits.

Gypsy VIII spiraled off in the spectacular blast with no incident and the crew went to work at once after passing our moon. They prepared experiments and checked and rechecked systems. It was a long trip out. They slept in shifts in bunks. They ate in shifts. They did daily physical exercises. They transmitted interviews with kids back home.

"Do you like space, Kelsey?" the first kid asked into the transmitter face.

"Yes, it's wonderful, you guys!" said Kelsey into the transmitter face. "Where are you from?"

"We're in Kentucky," said the first kid.

"Is it better than you thought?" said the next kid. "What does space feel like?"

"Yes, it's strange. It's light into my bones and head," said Kelsey Starr.

The kids laughed. "Like dizzy?"

"Not really dizzy," said Kelsey. "It's dark out here," she said. "Sort of like skating and swimming at the same time."

The kids laughed.

"What's your horse's name?"

"Buck and Candy. I have two."

"Are the meteors big?"

"Some are a quarter the size of our moon. They get smaller from there. Some are the size of Omaha if Omaha was a ball."

"Will you bring a flag?"

"No flags. It causes problems."

"What did you bring to space with you?"

"Books to read, my parents' picture, a pet rock."

"What color?"

"Brown." They laughed and laughed.

"Do you ever wear dresses?"

"Yes, of course."

"Are you scared?"

"Just enough to make us careful!" Kelsey Starr said. "Space is perfectly safe. We'll be perfectly fine."

Later, the kids all jumped on their gym mats. The teacher could not settle them down until an hour after lunch.

The crew physician said Kelsey should drink a protein shake, so she did in the galley. In the library she sent a message to her mom at 9 AM Lennox time and read a horse-racing report from Kentucky. She scheduled an interview with the Lennox High Science Club. She went to her bunk.

She tried to imagine what Roger Cotton would look like if they ever met.

> Hey Roger,
> Thanks for the essay on Time. Nice work! How the heck did you learn about my Poly Cal essay? You sure are a clever one! I'm writing this message on the Gypsy VIII transmitter, of course, the one under a crew bunk. My space walk is tomorrow. I'm excited. The mission is going very well. Remember, Roger, that things are always better than you think. People can switch and change. When I feel down, I just count up all the people who love me. Chin up and happy raking. I hope your finger is better! Guam sounds nice. Send me a post card when you go and thanks for the spice kit.
> Best always,
> Comm. Kelsey Starr
> Gyspy VIII Deep Space Explorer
> 1,335,357,880 km from Lennox, NB.
> PS: I finally met your wife. She's lovely. We had tea on campus. I told her about the amulet. I hope you don't mind.

"Who were you writing to?" asked Commander Sean Griffin, who glided in for sleep shift.

"A friend," said Kelsey Starr and punched off the transmitter under the crew bunk.

"What a smile, should I be jealous?" said Sean Griffin.

She held out a hand to him. He gave her a back rub.

They slept soundly in cocoons like baby mice.

Roger Cotton made two trips to Guam later in life. He always brought his bike. The handlebars has been retrofitted to serve his special needs, an issue of balance and steering.

The doctor's wife wouldn't allow surgical procedures in the house. The first time, the doctor rented a boat for the visit through PX connections for privacy. He brought his black bag with tools and suctions, ointments and gauzes in different sizes. The work on Roger Cotton was done in the galley unless the atmosphere was extremely hot. Roger drank vitamin water on the deck before being rowed ashore. The palm trees were taller in Guam than at the Omaha Zoo. Small night animals moved in black shrubs around the cove where the boat was moored, small but as hungry as bulls or cougars.

"I'm glad to be free of it finally, you know?" Roger Cotton would often say.

"Yes," the doctor would say.

"Everyone is a coward sometimes, I think," Roger would say.

"Yes."

There were spices galore in Gaum. It was a scented island, people said. Roger Cotton bicycled all over it.

Lennox High School Mascot Manual
1. Safety First
2. School Moral and Sportsmanship
3. The Beaver as Example

Her space walk to M.Flg45x-27:23 began at 7:23 AM in the tricky meteor cluster. The ship maneuvered over as close as possible. Kesley Starr was still required by unforeseen positioning issues to fly for 12 minutes and 39 seconds. She secured her harness to the subject meteor with three anchor clips that she drilled in with a toe-crank and got to work.

Her autonomous flight unit recorded the oxygen malfunction at 8:29 AM.

"Kelsey, something's up with your oxygen. Over."

"Roger that. My gooseneck scrubber is blown. Over."

"Kelsey can you secure the line? You are too far out for retrieval. Over."

"Negative. I can't reach it. Over."

"Kesley, this is the commander now. Can you secure your line? Over."

"Negative. I have a jam. The gooseneck valve is blown to bits. Over."

Kelsey Starr kicked her legs. She groped behind her.

She hopped on the meteor. She unclipped the first anchor.

"A retrieval crew is deploying, Kelsey. Did you get that? Over."

She bounced to the second anchor and unclipped. The meteor was a bouncing beach ball. She bounced and it bounced.

"Roger, that. It's so beautiful here. Over."

She threw the beach ball in the air, a slow ballet. Sean Griffin came on.

"Kelsey. Stay with us. We're coming. Over."

"It's a long way. Can't wait to see you. How did this happen? Damn it. Over."

Her breath was noisy. The commander came back on.

"I have to ask, Kelsey, do you want to initiate CODE? Negative or affirmative, Kelsey, on CODE? Please confirm Step 1. Over."

She opened her flight pack and pulled the coil of silver in her glove.

"Please confirm Step 1. Over."

CODE was designed for perfect recordation, transmission, reconfiguration and global composition of every cell in her body from toenail to ponytail, every thought, every memory, and mood. Every molecule relative to every other, and tendon, muscle, and organ, hormones and fluids by volume of blood in those famous veins, arteries, capillaries. Each follicle and curvilinear trajectory of skin, every blemish, bump, and cavity. The clog in the kidney that would cause problems with urination in 5.2 years. The minor infection in the throat that had ignited a cough two days into the mission, ovum number 264 that had just dropped down the fallopian tube ready to implant. The expansion of lungs, then discharging. The heart pumping as the lips changed from red to purple in gray space light. Each hairline and line of thought of memory of fact forgotten and remembered by recording in the brain, for hurling back through space to the nose of a satellite dish on a Hawaiian volcano, once dormant but now rumbling and snow-capped at such low latitude, to be flung on to Omaha and scribbled in the fresh tangled gray matter in the Omaha basement: I am Kelsey Starr. I see the space line of blue-brown meteor rising in the retina. I know who she loved best, mother or father. The horse and the field. Her crystal ball spinning silver and backward in the moments before cardiac arrest.

"What's that? Over," said Kelsey Starr.

The glove released Roger Cotton's amulet and chain. They floated above her head, an inch an hour toward a pretty, nameless nebula.

"Kelsey, can we confirm CODE? Over."

"Tell Roger I did it," said Kelsey Starr.

"Kelsey. Can we initiate CODE?"

"Tell Roger Cotton I released his object," Kelsey Starr said. "Tell him his object is now projectile in infinity forever. You copy that?"

"We copy."

"Great," said Kelsey Starr. "Tell everyone: friends need to help each other out."

"Kelsey. Standing by for affirmative on CODE Transmission. Kelsey, we need you to do this. We are standing by. Over."

"Can you get my mother on? Over."

She unclipped the last anchor.

She turned a somersault.

"Please confirm Step 1. Commander Starr. Please confirm. Over."

"I want to speak to my mother," said Kelsey Starr.

"We do not have time. Please confirm."

She pushed off the meteor in a new direction.

The mandatory CODE Note of Decision and Explanation by Ms. Kelsey Marie Starr was sealed and addressed to Belinda Starr. It was in a safe at Mission Control. It was handwritten on scented paper with lily pads in the corners in a matching envelope inside standard issue Air Force stationery, also sealed with real wax. The President wanted to read the letter on the National Day of Mourning, with the flags at half-mast, but it was election season and Belinda Starr was against the incumbent. She was especially against such transparent political maneuvers when her daughter's death was involved. Instead, Belinda Starr read part of her daughter's words, with some exclusions and edits for style, by candlelight to thousands in the Lennox courthouse square. Mrs. Starr was front and center. She wore a pretty flowered dress to demonstrate her attitude about her loss.

"I died how I wanted to," she read, "which is better than most anyone can say."

Jason Starr wore black beside Belinda and was too distraught to speak or read.

Mourners poured into town all that day. The gas stations and markets sold T-shirts for charity that said, "Never Forget," with Kelsey Starr's picture smiling over a map of the U.S.

surrounded by appliqué comets and ringed planets. The shirts were expensive but sold out in hours. Stars on sticks waved above the heads in every color with more Kelsey faces. She had not been pretty, but it hardly mattered. Mrs. Starr held the handwritten note up for the crowd. The people cheered and cried, embracing strangers.

Several bikes were stolen from the shrubbery during the Kelsey Starr event. A few lucky others lay on their sides on Main Street and First Avenue, as if abandoned by the culprit mid-crime. Still other bikes, equally carelessly parked, leaning and unlocked on trees or against parking meters, were spared altogether. "There was no rhyme or reason to it," said the police to the victims who reported the thefts after the candles were extinguished and smoke cleared and people began yawning and looking about them. The police wrote reports by their squad cars in the blocked-off streets until well past eleven. The out-of-town riffraff were blamed.

The crowd dissipated. The Lennox High Band played on beautifully, softly, as the mourners drifted to the edge of the square and stood in groups, talking and admiring the courthouse that was lit up with enormous spotlights on wheels that had been rented and trucked down from Kansas City. The carvings on the façade had an entirely different appearance that night than on any normal day or night, mysterious and ancient. The people went home to their beds but the golden lights beamed up at the marble columns all night long. An excess of light mounted into the sky. The golden cloud, in fact, could be seen for miles over the flatland, so bright that a traveler passing through the region, a stranger approaching Lennox from one of the several small dark highways that converged there, might have slowed at the crest of a hill outside town and parked on the shoulder to marvel at the burning glow.

He might even have checked his map, adjusted his in-
struments, dials and digits, reset his coordinates, awaited
recalculation and reconfirmation, for a moment mistaking
Lennox for a huge, important city.

Then confirmation would have come.

"Yes, indeed. Lennox at fifteen kilometers. And what a
fire it must be!"

The traveler might have pulled back on the highway and
coasted down the hill toward the light. Happy. He had not,
after all, lost his way.

Reptile House

Carl's wife lay back, sanitized stirrups biting at her heavy ankles. Ten centimeters. The steel edge under her spit out a baby. A pair of blue rubber gloves made the catch.

Carl's head had hovered between the suspended knees and witnessed the exit close up. A tunnel and black fist of hair. Then shoulders, tiny but slumped like an old man's, then the crooked little body came out thrashing, apparently wanting no part of this new light world. Carl could understand. The skinny legs slid out last, kicking hard with feet too small to take seriously. This baby was a messy smear, a victim of riot, when the good place turned inside out.

The face was embedded with a pair of eyes that roved, a sort of nose screwed in the middle, and a small mouth that was small but loud, like it belonged to a thing with a dial. A cord coiled into the place where Carl's wife was. Carl didn't like his wife much anymore, but he didn't know it yet.

"Carl, cut the cord," she said.

"Cut the cord," he repeated, and set a hand on the knee.

Carl didn't want to cut the cord. He had done it for the others and this, he felt, was more than his share. The other kids were tucked in and away for a few days at her sister's spread in Winnetka, not far from his parents' old farm. His own modest house off Cicero, just southwest of downtown, was enticingly empty tonight, all five windows to the street, three on top and two on each side of the red door, would be dark. He hoped to get home tonight and sleep some in the big empty bed, in all that still and lonesome.

The green nurse handed Carl the scissors and the scissors sliced through red and blue flesh. This done Carl stepped from between the legs and made way. Someone tied a small knot of independence.

"Carl, hold the baby."

Carl's arms took the baby, bounced it, pitied it, then gave it back. The TV bent down from the ceiling like a nun. A breathing machine, EKG on a cart, and devices Carl didn't know stood at ready for ON and OFF, breathe, don't breathe, live, don't live.

The doctor reached in and stitched Carl's wife with a black seam. The blue and green nurses huddled close as the thread pulled through. Sponges, syringes to blood and bruise. A wince and moan. When the baby first cried and everyone laughed.

One thing: the fluorescent in the ceiling fixture had flickered to almost out. This bothered Carl. Another thing: the breathing machine box was off plumb on the wall and irritating. Carl was in construction. He worked in the showroom of a leading building supply outfit, his boss having flown him for training in fasteners—now the go-to guy on this very subject. No excuse for sloppy work. Carl stared down the off angle.

"Carl, some water."

The plastic pitcher tipped and the water poured. "Straw?"

"Yes, a straw. You're a love, Carl." She tossed a kiss without looking. She was exhausted. She wore a baseball cap backwards on her disheveled head. She sipped on the straw while the baby sipped on her. Carl sipped on nothing. No one brought him water.

The baby was off for a bath and immunizations. Carl's wife dabbed cocoa butter on her wide brown nipples. Carl turned his back with the *Tribune* and folded into the crossword. There was nothing wrong with her at all. A mother. Wide hips, a smile, and a mind. "Heart of gold" was what people said, but these were just three words.

She had half-finished the puzzle in pen back when she still could concentrate, sometime between two centimeters and three. The puzzle was called "Creatures of Our World" and now Carl used a pencil. The empties, across and down, seemed glad to have his latest scratchings, starting with four letters down for "A dog without pedigree." Carl wrote M U T T in the boxes. She moaned in the bed, turned and moaned again. It was contagious because Carl moaned too. Sick, edgy, out of sorts. Carl.

"Carl!" she said.

"Yes, dear."

"Carl."

He went back to his puzzle.

"Disney's orphan deer," but she had beat him to it: B A M B I, five down in the bottom right.

If Carl could have been anything it would have been a long-haul truck driver. He would have gone by Jack for the snappy consonants and driven this Great Land in his shiny eighteen-wheeler. Driving fast and long miles with red eyes and a filled thermos. He'd have lived in that cab, slept in the space behind the seat with a propane cook stove and a satellite TV. He'd have dozed to the CB chatter while rainstorms and snowstorms blasted the windshield, Manifest Destiny served up with coffee and pie from girls with slim ankles and pink aprons. He would have dropped in at the house off Cicero from time to time for a little two-on-two with the boys, report cards, and hand over the paycheck.

An orange nurse came in with a clipboard and plumped his wife's pillow. "How are we, sweetie? Big night." His wife smiled, signed a few papers, and the orange nurse left.

A beat-up pigeon presided on the brick sill out the window. He liked it at first as it paced and pecked at nothing. It seemed pleasant and interested. It tapped the glass with its dirty beak from time to time. Carl thought it looked pregnant, but it was the wrong time of year. Just getting a lot to eat, lucky bird, born at the right place at the right time.

From the sill the pigeon could see a room with a man and crossword. A lady with brown nipples, rubbing them in circles, and looking at the doorway as if waiting for someone. A perfectly clean and empty trash can by the door under the light switch which was a small fixture, about the height of an infant's foot. The doorway opened and welcomed out. A hallway beyond was wide, cool and serene, leading to an elevator bay somewhere around the corner with a button pointing down to the foyer, where a reception desk was tended at this hour by a sleepy man with a handlebar mustache and a winter coat since the revolving glass doorway went around and around forever like a child's toy, perpetually offering the Outside to any taker, fresh air without end, and beyond this, if the bird turned and looked over the edge, was the shoveled walk to the parking lot, hooded streetlamps spraying light over all including the edge of a street beyond, a street to other streets, a clutter of streets which by and by rambled to a cloverleaf entrance ramp, around and around up and merging left to eight sprawling lanes and seventy miles per hour even in the middle, and many miles before it cinched down to six lanes, then four, until maybe in Iowa or Nebraska, there was a simple ramp off right and down to two lanes, with the double-dash for passing, yellow, a sloping shoulder to the perpetual ditch, and west to Elsewhere.

Carl's finger pulled a string and the blind rolled down. A pigeon can be eradicated that easily.

"Carl."

"Yes, love."

She needed to pee and he walked her elbow to the bath. She was five feet four inches, 135 lbs., light brown hair. That's what her driver's license said about her. Mrs. to the neighbor kids, Mom to her own and Carl, since her other name got stuck in his jaw sometime between the first and second child. A set of creases was forming around both of their mouths.

"Carl, did you call Daddy?"

"Not yet," said Carl. "It's too late. He'll be in bed."

"Of course you'll call."

The pay phone down in the hall had a seat and a folding door that closed. The quarters dropped and the finger dialed. Pull yourself together.

If he ever got a chance he would go to Catalina Island. He would be an old-fashioned man there, tall, stout, round as a rock, and reliable. Big hands and a big mouth. It was a beautiful place, he'd heard, just close enough to the continent that you could still see it, know it's there, but still give civilization the finger. Like paradise with orange trees, lemons and pomegranates everywhere you look. He read in a book there was a town where people pedaled one-speed bikes up and down the little roads to get milk and eggs from friendly neighbors and smell the flowers and apples day and night. Carl later learned there were cars and trucks on Catalina, ferries to the mainland, and phones to anywhere else too. So that book was out of date and wrong. He had never eaten a pomegranate except once in Sunday school.

His wife took something for pain below. Carl took something for pain in his head. He sat in a chair at the window, looking. At a crash down the hall, the blue nurse ran and Carl thought of crashes, the empty house, the level in his gas tank. The little white car. The baby slept, then woke, then slept. He grabbed the puzzle off the floor.

Five down. "Humped and never thirsty."

C A M E L. He wondered what the word would look like in Arabic or some language and place that did not have camels at all. It would not fit the white boxes. That was near certainty.

Once, before Carl had married, Carl's boss was on the showroom floor. He had seen Carl many times, but asked Carl's name anyway. "Carl," said Carl.

And the boss said, "Seems like someone was just mentioning something about you."

"Good or bad?" Carl asked excited.

"Very good. Whatever it was, I can't remember, but you are the very best at it."

Carl never heard.

"So hot in here," the wife's voice said. "Should we open the window?"

"Too cold for the baby," he said. Carl was cold, though he was never cold, a warm-blooded man. A cold snap. Snap out of it.

So cold, so sick, so out of sorts. At the showroom, he was cheerful and easy, the go-to guy for sticky situations and unhappy returns, the people with the warped beams, mismatched colors, the ratchet sets with missing ratchets. But now Carl wanted to zip out of his skin. On the bedside table was a bunch of daisies in a plastic cup tipped over and he could not set them right. Their heads leaned on a phone book three inches thick full of strangers and over a stack of seven identical postcards of the Sears Tower, already stamped and addressed to friends and family. "WATER BROKE AT WATER TOWER PLACE!! CRAZY! HERE WE GO AGAIN!!! XXX OOO!!!" The same message was printed on each.

Carl clicked the box for the TV and an old ball game came on. October 1963, and three guys were talking with no volume and the players wore old-fashioned uniforms that Carl almost remembered. When Carl was young he wanted to fly an airplane or be a forest ranger. He might have been a scientist like the one who discovered the 366th day, an Arab with an abacus and a stick for making marks in the desert sand, living in a stone room. A tray of wine and bread glided through a slot at sundown. Batter up, same as now. There's the pitch, a line drive to second, thrown out at first for a double play which retired the side. Like any modern team. The channel jumped. The La Brea Tar Pits are asphalt seeps smack in Los Angeles and one of the only archaeological sights in the world where predator fossils outnumber the prey. They were like black swimming pools, these pits. Carl had always planned to get a backyard built-in pool for the kids. For swimming. Above ground would do. Maybe if the bonus came in. The channel jumped, a helicopter over the Great Wall of China, coiling down, all those stones set by some poor man, like an old animal lounging on the land green and pretty. The channel jumped back to baseball, pop fly to center, but Carl did not see what became of it because the TV clicked off.

"Should we open the window?"

"Too cold for the baby."

Yesterday Carl had stood in line at a busy downtown post office and bought the book of postcard stamps at her bidding. Writing her cards in the waiting room, though, she had rejected these stamps he'd chosen. She'd taken his Forever Stamps instead, his pretty stamps with the Liberty Bell on them, F O R E V E R printed in vertical next to the bell. Carl had never heard of them, but the clerk at the big counter was hawking them hard, giving his pitch to every patron in line: "The Perpetual Stamp. First Class guaranteed at forty-one cents from this day forward and forever. Hell or high water. Never expires, never declines in value, even if letter rate goes to a million bucks. Great investment. How many books do you want?"

Carl had stood at the clerk's big counter thinking of Fate and Perpetuity: the Sears Tower, house paint and report cards. He was tired. He was hungry. When they had met many years ago, he'd said he liked the "gravity of her character," but he did not remember this feeling or what he had meant.

Flat line. Highway. An eighteen-wheeler could hold a lot of peanut butter, jugs of water, pilot crackers and rationing. Carl had bought three books of the special stamps.

His stomach growled and the pigeon scuffed around. His wife and the baby slept. Eight across for "The sea's diva." He scribbled S T A R F I S H and thought of Catalina Island, of the tide pools and urchins beckoning with delicate green arms. Once Carl left his wallet at work and had gone back in to find it after hours. The wallet was safe in the break room, but the day's cash deposit sat unattended in its dirty canvas bag by the till. A heavy bag too, since Friday was a big day at the showroom. That and a gallon of best red enamel came home with Carl that night. Barn Red, it was called, and high gloss. A new floor manager was fired soon after.

Six across: "Rodents in the Bard's title." Carl thought, erased, then wrote S H R E W S in boxes at the center of the puzzle. Good thing it was pencil. The words H Y D R A and E W E S made sense now and appeared.

Four down : "Places to keep animals." Carl's pencil wrote Z O O S, a word with a strange look, but so many words have that. W I F E, for example, or C A R L or L E A P. Look at them. Just lines and dashes cutting and crossing each other and promising sense. But phone lines made sense. Tunnels, conveyor belts. The double yellow, straight as an arrow across the desert in Arizona, made sense.

G O T O

Some time ago in the Reptile House at the zoo Carl watched a twelve-foot python open its big detachable jaws and swallow the other snake in the cage, its only companion. Black snake eats brown snake. Big snake eats little snake. Carl stood behind the glass eating peanuts from a bag. Two snakes became one as people flashed pictures, went running, and whispered with quick tongues in the echoing dark. His wife had stayed in the Big Cat House and had not seen the eating. The kids were at the dolphin show with the sitter. Had the snake made some sign before the deed? Some goodbye or explanation with those lidless eyes? Carl wanted to know, tried to remember. He'd witnessed it all.

To the guys at work he described how the final snake had two tails for a while, one pointing each direction, the gaping mouth in the middle, the brown tail flapping then still. Gulped shorter and shorter until gone. This was odd to see.

The zookeepers had said of the incident: "Unnatural, unprecedented, as far as we know." But Carl had doubted that. This was a PR statement if he ever heard one. But there are things zookeepers do not like to admit.

The pigeon tapped behind the blind and Carl thought how the snake would show that bird a time. His wife was not interested in reptiles. She did not like what Carl liked. Carl did not like what she liked either. Or other things too, so surprising with so little warning. He raised the blind and said this to the pigeon. His wife and baby slept far away, across the room, behind his back.

In the Reptile House, two windows down from the double snake in the cage, a nest of eggs had been hatching. The little things had tumbled in knots, striking and hissing, but it had been hard to take them seriously, until this.

Now the walls bleeped and whirred at him. Carl was hungrier. The two, his wife and baby, were a vague white bundle on the bed. At their elbows on a tray was an apple she'd bitten into at eight centimeters and abandoned, with lipstick and tooth marks in the green flesh, now in the sweet beginnings of rot. Apples are so good. Apples are historic and scientific in the morning on Catalina. There were no snakes on Catalina. Too far from shore.

He walked the apple to the trashcan. He stood in the door. He thought of going. There would be no traffic at this hour. Home fast, in the middle lane, going sixty-five to the turn at Cicero and leaving the tallest of the city behind. The windows would be dark, not ignoring dark, or oblivious dark, just sleeping dark, five of them, three on top and two in each side of the red front door, like a big glassy family. The frozen lawn would roll out flat for him and his legs would walk him home. And don't switch on the light. Keep it dark until tomorrow.

His wife stirred. "Maybe open the window."

"There's a pigeon out there."

"Don't be ridiculous, Carl."

When the window opened, the pigeon flew off. The green nurse came and took a pulse.

"You should go," said his wife. "We're alright without you."

"I'll be going," he said.

Carl put on his coat and found his keys. He grabbed the postcards and stamps. The elevator carried him down, the postcards slithered down the slot near reception, the revolving glass doors shoved him out to fresh air.

His keys clinked in the parking lot and the little car waited. A satellite beelined the blackness, bent toward the horizon. Like it was planning something big.

G R A V I T Y. Carl raised a hand up at it.

The parking lot, the side street, on-ramp, eight lanes, sixty-five miles per hour. The four-door whizzed away by the Lake, over the river, zigged and zagged by wharfs, beacons blinking, stone lions and white-capped waves, missiled through the tunnels of towers and past ballparks put to bed. Finally he zoomed under the massive central post office that squatted over the entire eight lanes like a big brick mother. Then the open road.

When Carl was a boy, the neighboring farm boarded horses. There was one young horse who was so tame they didn't tie him up or keep him in the paddock. The people just let the horse stand in the driveway or walk in the yard because he never went far from the house. He was too scared. But once on a full moon night, Carl had been walking the road, thinking of his future. At the neighbor's house, this horse came into view. It stood alone, a white shadow in that moon, and maybe not a real animal at all. Carl was startled at first, then recognized the horse and kept walking. This horse started to follow. Twenty feet back, then fifteen, then ten and Carl started getting scared. This horse had never been so far from the house before. And what if it was not the same horse, but a different horse of a different temperament? Or a different creature altogether? Young Carl found a tree and climbed up into it. The horse stood at the trunk until dawn and went home.

Carl's little white four-door whooshed past the Cicero exit. The fringe off the dirty berm swirled up like a laugh. Walls, corners and rooftops stacked high and low, marched on neat and trim. The billboards shouted and flashed: an umbrella, a mustache, a bottle of rum, as big as trees. Near the airport a cord of jets lashed fifty miles out over the Lake, heading past places like Kansas City or Maui, past landing strips and volcanoes with telescopes. A jet with landing gear slung low roared over the highway, and the little car flinched, swerved left, then righted itself to the middle lane.

Beyond the airport the city thinned and dimmed, private and pleasing. The billboards grew faint and quiet. The walls, corners and rooftops purpled and settled away lower and lower to the ground. The night split open. The car sped on.

The little car slowed for a bank of toll booths spanning the road that Carl did not remember. As the window rolled down and fingers fumbled for change, a pair of tall white lights, growing bigger, approaching fast, sprayed the rear window. The eighteen-wheeler purred to a standstill behind the little white car though all the other lanes, left and right, yawned entirely vacant. Its chrome face nuzzled in, steamed, licked closer until the grill grinned red in the taillights. It growled low at idle and the tollbooth shook as the quarters flew from Carl's hand, the nickel and two dimes too, and were gulped down. The white lights blinked to high beam blue. The gate snapped up, a green light said G O, and the little car went. The high beams winked a salutation as the car flew away around the next long curve.

In the dark, the white dashes dashed west and the little

car threaded between them. It was not long before the high beams came again bearing down fast from behind the long curve. Steady now, easy now. In the rearview mirror, the truck stalked closer, crept and reached, until, grasping, the little car was snared in a whizzing ball of light. Closer, closer, closer, the truck eased to looming within yards, within feet, inches of, and all was blue: the gripping hands, the trembling wheel, the shadow of the head on the dash. The dashes leapt on, the car, and the light, until at 84, something kissed the car's rear bumper, tenderly, and the shadow shook.

89 . . . 92 . . . 95.

Shortly, the others came too. They passed two from the left, one from the right, shiny black eighteen-wheelers, swirling rims and red rivets, without a single marking on their faces or flanks and no identifying plate or registration at the rear. The first of them slid from left into the lead, while the others sidled up even and cinched at the little car's sides, leaving no crack for daylight when daylight came. 97 shuddered through steel and rubber and Carl's mouth said something to no one in particular.

So it went for miles. The white slowed, the black slowed. The black surged, the white surged too. Nudge, bump, flinch, shove. Chrome fright roar bite knuckle knees teeth please faster stop faster please.

Boxed in.

The five lifted off at the border. If Carl's mouth made a noise, from a pink place in his lungs, it was a very small noise. They made good time in the dark, over the land and Lake that, by this time of night, was knocked over and licked up. To the rim and beyond it.

Acknowledgments

Many thanks to the editors of the journals in which the following stories have previously appeared:

Gargoyle: "For Swimmers";
The Carolina Quarterly: "Cold Snap";
The Common: "The Amazing Discovery and Natural History of Carlsbad Caverns";
Green Mountains Review: "Rabbit's Foot";
The Malahat Review: "No Name Creek";
The Nashville Review: "Reptile House".

I will ever be grateful to Peter Conners for finding, having faith in and improving this collection, to Jenna Fisher, Melissa Hall, Sandy Knight, and all the BOA staff and supporters for their hard work and vision in making the book ready for the world.

I owe an incalculable debt to Chris Bachelder, who guided the collection into being, also to Noy Holland, Sabina Murray, Jim Shepard, John Vinduska, Gloria Barrigan, Sandra Jenson, Michael Carolan, Scott Salus, and Tim Sutton, all who, in one way or another, were essential in inspiring, crafting, and refining these stories.

I am grateful to too many friends and family to list, from old worlds and new ones. Please accept my thanks, all of you, for your wisdom, fun, and faith. Thanks especially to Nancy Wainwright, Saunders McNeill, Betsy Hopkins, Peter Corbett and family, who were with me through the writing.

Finally, thanks to Margaret Eagleton and Mike Wissemann, my three sisters and my parents, for their bottomless support and love.

About the Author

Robin McLean was a lawyer then a potter for fifteen years in the woods of Alaska before leaving to pursue her MFA at UMass Amherst in Massachusetts. Her first collection, *Reptile House,* was a finalist for the Flannery O'Connor Short Story Prize in 2011 and 2012. McLean's stories have appeared widely in such places as *Western Humanities Review, Cincinnati Review, Carolina Quarterly, Nashville Review, Malahat Review, Gargoyle, The Common,* and *Copper Nickel,* as well as the anthology *American Fiction: The Best Unpublished Short Stories by Emerging Writers.* She currently teaches at Clark University and splits her time between Newfound Lake in Bristol, New Hampshire, and a 200-year-old farm in western Massachusetts.

BOA Editions, Ltd. American Reader Series

No. 1   *Christmas at the Four Corners of the Earth*
         Prose by Blaise Cendrars
         Translated by Bertrand Mathieu

No. 2   *Pig Notes & Dumb Music: Prose on Poetry*
         By William Heyen

No. 3   *After-Images: Autobiographical Sketches*
         By W. D. Snodgrass

No. 4   *Walking Light: Memoirs and Essays on Poetry*
         By Stephen Dunn

No. 5   *To Sound Like Yourself: Essays on Poetry*
         By W. D. Snodgrass

No. 6   *You Alone Are Real to Me: Remembering Rainer Maria Rilke*
         By Lou Andreas-Salomé

No. 7   *Breaking the Alabaster Jar: Conversations with Li-Young Lee*
         Edited by Earl G. Ingersoll

No. 8   *I Carry A Hammer In My Pocket For Occasions Such As These*
         By Anthony Tognazzini

No. 9   *Unlucky Lucky Days*
         By Daniel Grandbois

No. 10   *Glass Grapes and Other Stories*
         By Martha Ronk

No. 11   *Meat Eaters & Plant Eaters*
         By Jessica Treat

No. 12   *On the Winding Stair*
         By Joanna Howard

No. 13   *Cradle Book*
         By Craig Morgan Teicher

No. 14   *In the Time of the Girls*
         By Anne Germanacos

No. 15   *This New and Poisonous Air*
         By Adam McOmber

No. 16   *To Assume a Pleasing Shape*
         By Joseph Salvatore

No. 17   *The Innocent Party*
         By Aimee Parkison

Colophon

BOA Editions, Ltd., a not-for-profit publisher
of poetry and other literary works, fosters readership
and appreciation of contemporary literature.
By identifying, cultivating, and publishing
both new and established poets and selecting authors
of unique literary talent, BOA brings high-quality
literature to the public. Support for this effort comes from
the sale of its publications, grant funding, and private
donations.

The publication of this book is made possible, in part,
by the special support of the following individuals:

Anonymous x 2
June C. Baker
Rome Celli & Elizabeth Forbes
Gwen & Gary Conners
Michael Hall
Jack & Gail Langerak
Boo Poulin, *in honor of Jack Morrissey*
Cindy W. Rogers
Deborah Ronnen & Sherman Levey
Steven O. Russell & Phyllis Rifkin-Russell

3 1901 05776 0680